TRAIL
TO
HOME

JIM EDD WARNER

ISBN: 979-8-9865029-4-6 (Paperback)

Cover designer: GetCovers
Graphic designer: Deborah Stocco

Other books in The Rampy Family series by the author:
Trail from New Orleans to Santa Fe (book 1)
Trail to New Orleans (book 2)

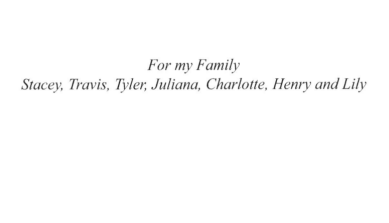

For my Family
Stacey, Travis, Tyler, Juliana, Charlotte, Henry and Lily

TABLE OF CONTENTS

Prologue 5

1 | Albuquerque 7

2 | Fiona's Home 14

3 | The Hotel...25

4 | Volcano..35

5 | Trouble in Town 41

6 | Leaving Albuquerque 52

7 | To Chihuahua 61

8 | Chihuahua 75

9 | Heading to the Sea 89

10 | Sailing from Matamoros 100

11 | Through the Storm.......................................112

12 | New Orleans..129

13 | Trail to Home 146

14 | Leaving New Orleans....................................155

15 | The Canyon 169

16 | Trail to Home 181

PROLOGUE

Troy Rampy, a merchant from New Orleans, and his brothers Don and Aubrey, recently completed a trip with other merchant friends to Santa Fe in New Spain. They had taken wagons loaded with assorted goods from New Orleans and St. Louis across-country in mule-drawn wagons. The year was 1821.

Troy's youngest brother, Bill, had ridden to Santa Fe previously to investigate the area for business opportunities. Bill not only found strong business opportunities and ties; but also, a beautiful young woman to spend his life with. Frances and Bill were married by her brother when Bill returned to Santa Fe with his brothers and their merchant friends.

Bill had left Frances with her family, where he had met them, in Chihuahua, the previous winter. His hope had been to return to Chihuahua as soon as he could, after reporting back to Troy about Santa Fe business prospects.

Luckily, when Bill and the rest of his group got to Santa Fe, Frances and her family were there watching her brother be installed as a priest in the Santa Fe Parish. Bill had anticipated needing to go on to Chihuahua before he would see her again. That trip would have been an additional five hundred miles, so seeing her in Santa Fe was like a miracle.

Troy and his friends had all sold their dry goods in Santa Fe, within a few days after arriving there. Some of the friends returned to the United States soon after they sold their goods. Troy and his brothers decided to follow Bill and his new family as far as Albuquerque, then stop there for a week or two, before returning to the United States.

Bill had suggested Albuquerque to Troy as a possible place for another store. He said the town seemed to be growing rapidly and was centrally located. He thought it was especially well-suited to serve trappers and prospectors heading west to the Rocky Mountains.

Troy, Bill, Don, and Aubrey had four sisters, who were still in Alabama where the siblings had all grown up. Their mother and dad were both from immigrant families and each spoke several languages. English, Spanish and French were the languages the kids grew up speaking most often around the farm, so being in New Spain was comfortable for all four of the brothers.

At this point. Spain had ruled Mexico for 300 years. It was just about to lose control over the country. After years of fierce battle between the two, Mexico was on the brink of becoming an independent country. Many traders from the U.S., including the Rampys, had been planning trade trips to Mexico, since Mexico's independence seemed to be at hand.

1 | ALBUQUERQUE

Bill Rampy had just bumped into his brother, Troy, on the main street of Albuquerque. Troy had just come out of a clothing store. He had been talking to the store owner about new trade opportunities in the area. "Troy, what are you and the guys planning to do after you leave here? Frances and I would love for you to come to Chihuahua and spend some time with us."

Troy said, "Bill, I think we would love that too; but first, I would like to spend more time here in Albuquerque and get to know this area better. From what I have seen, so far, and what you have told me, it sounds like a great place to do business. It is at the junction of at least two important trade routes. And the traffic on those routes promises to keep growing."

The town itself is obviously growing. Once we have spent a little more time here, we will come see you and Frances and her family. When will all of you be leaving for Chihuahua?"

"We should be leaving early the day after tomorrow. At least that is the last thing I heard from Frances' mother, Anita. They have been spending a lot of time with all the family living in the Albuquerque area and are about ready to go. It has been fun meeting Frances' relatives. I knew she had relatives in Santa Fe. I had no idea she had even more relatives in Albuquerque.

Bill added, "Her family has relatives that have been in or near Albuquerque since before it was founded in 1706. They do not think they are related to the Duke of Albuquerque, for which the town was named; but she is not certain. The Duke apparently never came to New Spain to see the city named after him. He may have had relatives amongst the immigrants who settled here."

"I did not realize the town was that old, Bill, although, I should have guessed after looking at some of the architecture. The church is beautiful. I would not have guessed it to be over 100 years old."

"It's got to be close to that, at least from what Frances' relatives tell me."

"I'll talk to Don and Aubrey and let them know when you are leaving," Troy said. "We will see you off when you roll out. Then we will spend more time here in town and around the area. I anticipate that should take ten days to two weeks. Then we will head to Chihuahua."

"That would be great, Troy. I will let Frances and her parents know.

"Oh, Troy, speaking of Frances' relatives, there is going to be a meal for everybody tonight. You and the guys are invited. It will be at Aunt Fiona's house, on the west side of town. We can all go together. Meet us at the hotel at 4:00 pm."

"That sounds good. And I am sure Don and Aubrey will think the same thing. We may have to work at getting cleaned up a little. This sleeping by a campfire probably does not make a guy very ready for socializing."

"I am sure you will be alright, whatever you do. Remember, we are all pretty much in the same boat, except for the few who have been staying with relatives or at the hotel."

Troy laughed and said, "Yep, you are right about that. We will be looking forward to the supper and seeing everybody. We will meet you at the hotel."

Don and Aubrey were at their campsite near the river when Troy found them. They were working on the one remaining wagon still in their possession. The other wagons had been sold. Selling the wagons was not originally their intention, but the wagons were needed by almost every merchant they had talked to.

This remaining wagon was loaded with some of their own items, mainly wedding gifts given to Bill and Frances by relatives and friends in Santa Fe. Since Bill and Frances would be leaving them here in Albuquerque, the wagon would go with them. It was in good shape already, but the guys wanted to make sure nothing would go wrong with it on the trip to Chihuahua.

"Hi, Troy," Aubrey said as he saw their brother approaching. "What have you been up to this morning?"

"Oh, I have just been visiting with a few store owners to get to know some people. And I met Bill. He said Frances' Aunt Fiona has invited us for supper tonight. I told Bill that we would be glad to come. I was certain you two would not turn down a free meal."

Aubrey and Don both laughed.

"Bill told me that they will all be leaving for Chihuahua the morning after next. I figured we would try to see them off when they leave. I told him we would meet them at the hotel to go to Aunt Fiona's. Our plan is to meet at 4:00 pm and walk there together. She lives on the west edge of town. Bill told me how to get there if we should happen to miss them, so I do not think that should be a problem. I would rather go with them. We will need to ask more about the area west of her house a few miles. I understand there are some interesting ruins or artifacts we should see before we leave. "

"Oh," Aubrey asked, "What are they supposed to be like?"

"Not sure, Aubrey, but it is supposed to be in an area where there was a large volcanic eruption many years ago. The native people living in the area, after the eruption, carved or drew figures on the rocks as decorations or symbols of some kind. There apparently are thousands of them. The area is so large that we will not be able to see much of it, but we can certainly see a good sample."

"That sounds interesting," said Aubrey. "I would like to see some of it, even if it is way too big to see the whole thing. We will just have to see the rest when we come back."

"How are the repairs coming on the wagon? Will it be in good shape for Bill to take to Chihuahua?"

"Yeah, I think it is about as good as we can get it, Troy. Don and I have put all the skill we have into it. I would not want to claim it is as good as it was when it was new, but it is sturdy. It should get to Chihuahua okay."

"That is great, guys. I appreciate you doing that. I would not want Bill and his new bride to break down between here and home. I know they will have friends and family with them to help if need be. I would like them to have a trip without any problems.

"Hey, I have got another business I want to stop by and then I'll be back here to clean up a little before we go to Frances' aunt's house for supper. I will see you both in a little while."

Both Don and Aubrey said, "See you soon," as Troy walked away. Then they returned to putting a few finishing touches on the wagon. Don carved "Bill and Frances Rampy" into the seat of the wagon while Aubrey gave the wagon an extra good cleaning.

While Don and Aubrey finished the wagon, Troy went back to the plaza area. He had met a shopkeeper on the street south of the plaza that he wanted to talk to more. Justine Martinez had a small shop that supplied clothes, writing materials and houseware items to the locals. Her husband, Radalfo, and she had started the store seven years before. Three years later, Radalfo was killed in an accident. Soon after, their only child, Karina, was born. Justine had been running the shop and raising Karina by herself since then.

Troy had heard from other businesspeople in town that Justine was a good businessperson and well-liked by everyone in town. Her leadership skills were well known in the area.

"Mrs. Martinez, how are you today," Troy said, as he entered her store.

"Fine, thank you. And please call me Justine, Mr. Rampy."

"Fair enough, Mrs. Martinez. I will call you, Justine, if you call me Troy."

"That sounds good, Troy. And how are you today?"

"I am good. My brothers and I have been having a pleasant time here in Albuquerque. It is such a beautiful area and is filled with many pleasant people, like yourself."

"Thank you, Troy. I am glad you like it here. I have lived here for most of my life, and I like it too. Of course, I do not have much to compare it with. Well, except Santa Fe and Chihuahua. I think they are both nice too. But, to me, there is something special about Albuquerque. I love the way it sets here in the river valley with mountains on both sides. And I like the way the valley stretches out to the north and south. I love the style of architecture with the adobe buildings. But the people are my favorite part of this area. I guess they should be since I am related to most of them."

"That is the way it was back home in Alabama, where I grew up. We did not actually have an organized town like Albuquerque. It was more of a farm community where there were several dozen farm families scattered around relatively close to each other. We were related in some way or the other to most of them. And if we were not related to them, we still knew them. The nearest businesses were about twenty miles away. But the county seat, where there were more and larger businesses, was about forty miles."

"I have no idea how far Alabama is from here. It sounds like a long way, especially since I have never heard of it before. What brought you and your brothers to this area?"

Troy laughed and said, "It's too long a story to tell you today, but I would like to tell you sometime." He paused and finally said, "I guess the short story is that I am a businessman from New Orleans. Last year, my brother, Bill, came to Santa Fe to see if it would be a good place to do business. He came back to New Orleans, and we agreed that we should get several wagon-loads of merchandise and take them to Santa Fe. We did and sold everything we brought. Now my other two brothers that came with us and I are spending a couple of weeks in the Albuquerque area. Then we will follow our brother Bill to Chihuahua. From there we will go back to New Orleans."

"That does sound like a story I would like to hear, Troy. You will have to come back and tell me some day before you leave."

"I will. We should be here at least ten days or so. I will be back to see you before we head toward Chihuahua. That is a promise."

Troy and Justine said their goodbyes and Troy headed back to get together with Aubrey and Don. Troy had walked to Justine's shop and was tired by the time he got back to their camp. Don and Aubrey had spent more time making sure the wagon was ready for Bill and Frances.

As Troy walked up to them, Aubrey said, "Troy, what did you find out today?"

Troy, with a thoughtful look on his face said, "Actually nothing. I went to see Justine Martinez, intending to talk about Albuquerque business in general. I hear that she is one of the best business people in the area and well respected by her customers and other shopkeepers as well."

"So, why didn't you learn anything? Would she not talk to you?"

"No, Aubrey, that is not it. We talked. I just never got around to talking to her about business or Albuquerque."

"What did you talk about then?"

"Each other, I guess. She told me about growing up in Albuquerque and I told her about growing up in Alabama."

Don, who walked up about that time asked, "Did you tell her about your wild sailing adventures, after you left home?"

"I do not think so. We mainly just talked about family and home."

"It sounds like you were on a date, not a business meeting," Aubrey said. "So, tell me Troy, what did Justine look like?"

Troy, with an odd smile said, "Well, it certainly was not a date. Justine is an especially charming woman. She is tall and slender and has beautiful auburn hair."

Don laughed as he was changing his shirt for supper and said, "Well, it may not have been a date, but I think you should stay away from her shop, or we'll be coming back here for another wedding soon."

Troy gave sort of a half chuckle and started getting busy cleaning up for the gathering. The odd smile on his face took quite a while to fade away.

When all three of them were ready, they headed to the hotel. It was a new hotel, so Bill and Frances had decided to stay there for a few nights instead of with family since Frances' parents were staying with Aunt Fiona.

2 | FIONA'S HOME

Bill and Frances had just finished talking with an old friend of Frances in the hotel lobby when Troy, Don, and Aubrey walked in. Frances and Bill, both waved them over to give them hugs and introduce them. Frances said, "Troy, Don, and Aubrey, I want you to meet my friend, Dolores. Dolores, these gentlemen are Bill's brothers."

Turning to the guys, she said, "Dolores and I went to school together when we were small. She and her husband, Umberto, moved to Albuquerque from Chihuahua several years ago. They are running the hotel now."

Troy said, "Dolores, it is a pleasure to meet you."

She said, "It is nice to meet you. Frances said that you are going to Chihuahua with them and then back home in the United States. I am sure that it will be a long trip. What do you do in the United States?"

"I have a dry goods store in New Orleans," Troy said. "I am thinking about opening a store here in Albuquerque. Aubrey, Don, and I will go to Chihuahua after spending another week or two here, to get to know the area better. After we spend some time in Chihuahua, we will go back to New Orleans."

Frances said, "Dolores, it was wonderful to see you and Umberto again. It has been way too long. Hopefully, we will see you more often in the future."

"I would love that, Frances. I hope you have a nice time at your Aunt Fiona's. Tell her I sent my love to her."

"I certainly will. See you soon."

With that, the five of them headed to Fiona's home. It was a beautiful day. There was just enough wind to gently carry the dust away, as they walked.

Fiona's home was a large adobe house with a log porch across the front. There was a smaller log porch on the back. The house was surrounded by tall cottonwood trees. Fiona lived in the house with her husband, Jesse, and their four daughters: Gloria, Gala, Larisa, and Gabriella.

As Frances and the other four walked up the stairs onto the front porch, Fiona rushed out of the house and grabbed Frances. She said, "Frances, it is wonderful to see you and Bill again, so soon. And Bill, these must be your brothers," she said looking at Troy and the other two.

"Yes, these is my brothers Troy, Aubrey, and Don. Troy is the oldest and I am the youngest. And, of course, the other two just fall in the middle somewhere."

They all laughed. Aubrey said, "Thanks for your respect, Bill." He turned to Fiona and said, "Hi Aunt Fiona. I am Aubrey. I am next to Troy in age."

Fiona said to the group, "Gentlemen, I am honored to have you all in my home for supper. I hope you enjoy your time here. There are several more family members already here and a couple who have not arrived yet. Please make yourself at home." She opened her front door and ushered everyone into the front room.

Frances went around the room introducing Bill to those who had not met him yet. Then she introduced Troy, Aubrey, and Don to the group.

Coming back into the room, Fiona said, "It should be about forty-five minutes before supper is ready, so everybody, please relax. Please get to know Bill and his brothers if you have not already met them."

Troy went back out on the porch, just as two more people walked up the front steps. He was surprised to see Justine Martinez and her daughter.

Aubrey and Don were following Troy onto the porch, but turned around to go the other way when Troy said, "Justine Martinez, what a pleasure it is to see you again."

Justine had a surprised look on her face, when she said, "Troy Rampy, what are you doing here? I got a note from Aunt Fiona that she was having family over for supper. Are you part of the family now? I think I remember telling you that I was related to almost everybody in town. So, I guess this is proof. Oh, and let me introduce you to my daughter, Karina." She turned to Karina and said, "Sweetheart, this is Mr. Troy Rampy. He is from the United States."

Troy gave her a big smile and said, "Karina, it is a pleasure to meet you."

Just then, Aunt Fiona rushed out onto the porch to give Justine and Karina big hugs. She said, "I hope you have both had a good day. Justine, I know you work so hard. I hope you can relax for a while and enjoy the supper I have prepared." Turning to Troy, she said, "Have you met Troy Rampy? He is one of the brothers of Frances's husband, Bill."

Justine said, "I have met Troy, but I hadn't made the connection between him and Bill yet."

Aunt Fiona said, "I'll let you two get better acquainted while I go put the finishing touches on supper."

Justine turned to Troy with a smile on her face and said, "What do you know, we are almost related."

They both laughed and Troy said, "I guess so. How did that happen?"

"You tell me, Troy. How did it happen? Somehow, I feel you know a lot more about this story than I do."

"Well, I guess there is one more story, I should tell you," Troy said. "Actually, it is all part of the same story."

Just then, Aunt Fiona called that supper was ready, and everyone started moving toward the dining room.

"I guess the story will have to wait," Troy said.

"Ok, but just for a little while. I have got to hear this. Maybe we can sit together at supper and continue our conversation?"

"I think that would work. I have a feeling that Bill and Frances will be telling most of the same story," Troy said. They both moved toward the dining room. Karina had found some of the other young people and was going to eat with them on the back porch.

Supper was arranged in large dishes along the top of a beautiful wooden credenza in the dining room. Bill and Frances got to go first, and then the children. When Troy and Justine got their plates full, they moved back into the living room and ate over a low table there.

Troy assumed they would need to return to the dining room soon when Aunt Fiona introduced Bill and Frances. However, most of the guests had met them over the past few days as the newlyweds made their rounds in Albuquerque with Frances' parents.

As Troy and Justine began to eat, Justine said, "Ok, Troy, so tell me what I don't know about you and Bill, and Frances' relationship with Bill, and anything else I should know."

Troy laughed and started into his story. "As I have already told you, I grew up in the hills of eastern Alabama with three brothers and four sisters. Bill is the youngest brother. And next to me, he is probably the most adventuresome. Our other two brothers, Aubrey, and Don, are here tonight. I will introduce them to you after supper.

"I am the oldest and left home first. I traveled to the east coast of the U.S. and decided to work on a sailing ship. I worked on several different ships that sailed up and down the coast moving trade goods from town to town, and to many different dealers. I found it enjoyable once I got used to the constant movement of the ships.

"I made a close friendship with another person who went to work sailing at the same time I did. You may know him. His name is Juan Leos."

"Know him? I am related to him also," Justine interjected. "I told you I was related to everybody. This story keeps getting more interesting by the minute. Excuse me for interrupting, Troy. Please continue."

"Once Juan and I had sailed for about a year and a half, the ship we were on got caught by a terrible storm. It lasted for three days. With every man working almost constantly as hard as he could, we were able to escape the storm and get to land.

"After that storm, Juan and I decided our careers as sailors were over. Juan went back to Santa Fe and started a trading post. I went to New Orleans and started a dry goods store.

"A couple of years later, Bill came to visit. I asked him to stay and work with me. He stayed and was a great help to me. We eventually got to talking about Mexico and their war for independence from Spain. It seemed to us that Santa Fe merchants might be good to trade with, since the war appeared to be coming to an end. Bill volunteered to go to Santa Fe and get to know some merchants in the area.

"Of course, I asked him to look up Juan to see how he was doing. Once he got to Santa Fe, he found some relatives of Juan's who told him how to find Juan's trading post. They became good friends immediately and Juan asked him to stay and work at the trading post for a while. That led to them going together to the trade fair in Chihuahua."

"Oh, I think I am beginning to get part of the picture," Justine said.

"Yes, as you have already probably guessed," Troy continued, "Juan introduced Bill to his relatives in Chihuahua. Bill
and Frances got to know each other, and decided they should
spend their lives together. However, he had promised to return
to New Orleans to tell me what kind of business opportunities
he found in Santa Fe. With their promises of love and a desire
to marry when he turned, Bill left Chihuahua and made his way
back to New Orleans.

"I really thought he had more sense than that," Troy laughed.
"If I had been him, I would have married her and brought her
back to New Orleans. But the gentleman he is, Bill felt she
should stay safe with her family until he could go to New Orleans to see me. Then he would go back to her in Chihuahua."

"Oh, Troy," Justine said, "I think it was sweet of Bill to leave
Frances safely with her family. After all, it can be a dangerous
world out there."

"Yes, it certainly can," said Troy. "In fact, that reminds me
of another story you should hear. However, II am not the person
to tell it to you. Bill will have to tell you that story. It involves
an Indian attack."

Justine started to say something and then stopped. Then with
a tear running down her cheek, Justine said, "I think, I have
already heard some of that story and I am not sure I want to hear
any more. But, someday, maybe I will ask him about the attack."

Troy remembered the two men killed in the attack had
both been from Albuquerque. Justine obviously knew them or
perhaps was even related to them. "Justine, I'm sorry I even
mentioned that."

With difficulty she said, "That's ok Troy. I am just a little
sensitive when it comes to that incident. The two Albuquerque
men killed were good friends of my late husband. Their deaths
affected me a lot. And the wound of Radalfo's death is still too
fresh in my mind after all these years. So, I guess I cannot think
of one death without thinking of all three."

"I am sorry, Justine." Troy laid his hand on her arm.

She said, "Thank you, Troy," and happened to notice a tear on his cheek.

After an awkward, few minutes, Justine said, "Troy, did you come back with Bill when he returned to Frances, or have you come since then?"

"Yes, I came back at the same time. We put together a caravan that came at the same time. Merchant friends from St. Louis and our brothers, Don and Aubrey, all came with Bill and me."

Justine said, "You must have sold everything before you got here. I have not seen many new wagons around town, except for the ones taking wedding gifts back to Chihuahua."

"All of the merchandise brought with us was sold in Santa Fe. Our merchant friends left from there and headed straight back to St. Louis. They plan to come back again next year. Aubrey, Don, and I decided we would come to see Albuquerque before heading back to New Orleans. Bill told us we might want to start a dry goods store here. I think he was right. This looks like a good place to start another store. We could be of service to traffic going through town, both north and south, and to groups and individuals going to the mountains in the west."

"I think that is a good idea," Justine said.

Troy added, "I think the stores here now are doing a good job for the local families. We would hope to add to some of the capacity they have already and then do more to sell to travelers. Heavier equipment, wagons, trapping gear and maybe some agricultural machinery would be more our major line of work.

"Bill has talked me into following them to Chihuahua. I told him we would, after another week or two here. They are leaving the morning after next. I suppose we will spend a week or two there, to see if we can help them settle in. After that I intend for us to head back to New Orleans."

Justine said, "That sounds interesting, Troy. Will you go back the way you came?"

"No, I do not think so. We came by way of St. Louis, so there is no need to go that direction. I have been thinking about going by ship. My taste for sailing ships has never completely gone away, so going by water would be thrilling. We would probably follow the Rio Grande River down to its mouth. From there we would find the nearest port and catch a ship. Hopefully, we can find one straight to New Orleans. Of course, I realize we may have to wait a while."

Justine was looking especially interested when Troy mentioned sailing. She said, "I have always wanted to sail. My ancestors came to this country by ship. I envy them for that opportunity. Oh, maybe someday I will get to sail. So, what will you do once you get to New Orleans? Will you load up some merchandise from your other store and then come back?"

"I am not sure, Justine. I would like to do that. I have two partners back in New Orleans. I will have to talk to them and see what their intentions are. They may be tired of running the store and want me to buy them out. Or they may want to buy me out. That might be my preference. It will depend on what the situation is when I get back there. My store in New Orleans is nice. I never thought I would want to leave it; but this journey with my brothers, out to this different part of the world, has changed me. It seems to have awakened my old adventurer's spirit. I think I would not mind changing a few things about my life."

"That would certainly be a big step, Troy."

"Yes, I know it would be. But there is something intriguing about this area. It has its own beauty that is just overwhelming." Troy said these last few words as he was gazing fixedly at Justine. It was impossible for him to not notice the glow of her own beauty. He was falling in love with this country; but with her also.

Just then, Karina came over and jumped up in her mother's lap. She said, "It is getting late, Mommy. Can we go home?"

Justine smiled at her daughter and said, "Yes dear, we will go home soon. We should go tell Aunt Fiona that we had a wonderful time, and we hope to see her again soon."

She turned to Troy, touched him lightly on the arm and said, "Troy, it was nice to visit with you. I hope to see you again soon."

"Justine, it was a pleasure to talk to you. I will see you soon."

Justine and Karina walked toward the kitchen. They talked to every person they passed on the way, there and back. They both stopped for especially big hugs from Frances and Bill. As the guests of honor, Bill and Frances had most of the family in the house gathered around them.

Troy found Aubrey and Don. They had both been in a deep conversation, in Spanish, with Fiona's husband, Jesse. Their talk was concerning the area west of their home where there were thousands of pictures drawn on stones by ancient people who lived in the area. The volcanic rocks had been scattered over the ground thousands of years before.

Aubrey said, "Troy, come set down. We have been having the most interesting conversation with Jesse. He has been telling us about the field of volcanic rocks west of here. We really need to see them before we leave. Jesse said he would take us if we wanted him to. But he also said we can do it by ourselves. There apparently are so many rocks with pictures that you cannot miss them."

"There are hundreds or maybe thousands of them," interjected Don. "The rocks were decorated by both earlier immigrants and native people. Over here by the wall is a small rock like we are talking about. It does not have a picture because Jess did not think it would be right to bring home one with an etching. He said it appears to be a sacred place to the people who were here before. He has never seen any Indians in the area around there, so assumes they still hold it as sacred."

"How are you guys?" Bill asked as he walked into the room. "Jesse told us he had been telling you about the volcanic rocks with the etchings. That is especially interesting. Frances and I spent a little time out there yesterday. She had seen them several times before and found them fascinating. But if you go out there, be careful. It was warm yesterday and we saw several rattlesnakes out sunning themselves. They were big ones too."

"Oh, we will be careful," Aubrey said. "I never have liked to be around snakes, especially rattlesnakes. They are just too evil looking. And I have seen a few bites they gave people and the bites looked evil too."

"Tomorrow Frances and I and her parents are going to finish getting together the things we are taking on to Chihuahua. So, we will be around the hotel. What are you guys going to do? Will you go look at the volcanic area or put that off until we leave?"

"We will leave that until after you are gone," Troy said. "Aubrey and Don have the wagon finished, so we will bring it over to you. Will you have enough people in your group that someone can drive the wagon?"

"I'm not entirely sure, Troy," Bill said. "Frances and I will have to think through that with her parents."

Don said, "If you do not have a driver, we can drive it down there for you. After you get it loaded, we can take it back to our camp and add a few pieces to the load. It probably would be good for us to have some space in the wagon anyway. I had been wondering if we would need to get a packhorse to carry some of our gear. We do not have all that much, but some of it is bulky. We can get a packhorse in Chihuahua when we leave for New Orleans."

Bill said, "I have a feeling that it would help us if you guys take the wagon. I will talk to the family, and we can decide tomorrow, as we are finishing up the loads."

"That sounds good, Bill. We will see you at the hotel in the morning. Now, Don, Aubrey and I will go say our goodbyes to Fiona and Jesse and head back to camp."

"We will see you guys in the morning, Troy. Thanks for your help."

Troy led the way into the kitchen to speak to Fiona. He said, "Fiona, it was a wonderful meal. Thank you so much for inviting us over. You made us feel like a part of your family."

"Well, Troy, you gentlemen are part of the family now. It was a pleasure to have you here. Frances told me that you intend to spend two more weeks in the area before you follow them down to Chihuahua. I want you to know that the three of you have an open invitation to come back anytime for a meal. In fact, I want you to come back for supper again before you leave. As the time for your departure comes close, we will set a date."

"Fiona, that would be wonderful," Troy said. "We would love to see you again."

"And I will invite Justine and Karina over too if that is alright with you. I really do not have her over enough and you two seem to have already become friends."

"Fiona, that would be great. I do not know Justine well, but I can tell she is a wonderful lady."

"She certainly is Troy. And she is smart too. After her husband died, I know it must have been difficult for her to continue the store. She did it and never blinked an eye. And she is raising her lovely daughter Karina to be a good person too."

"Fiona, thanks again," said Troy. "We had better get back to our camp. We will keep in touch."

After a quick stop by the main table to speak to Frances and her parents, the three of them were headed back to camp. Tomorrow will be a busy day.

It was a beautiful evening. As the sun had gone down, the moon rose in the sky. It was almost full. The sky was clear enough that stars could be seen in every direction. The mountains to the east and west were clearly visible and made an impressive sight.

3 | THE HOTEL

The next morning, just as the sun was rising, Troy, Aubrey and Don were up having coffee around a small campfire. Growing up they did not give a thought to the size of a campfire. Their home was surrounded by wooded areas with endless fuel for fires. Now, living at times on the prairie or desert had taught them not to waste the precious fuel they needed for a fire.

Also, having trouble with those who wanted to harm them, had taught that a small fire was less visible and would not give their location away as quickly. Sometimes, cooking or heating was a little slower than they would like, but that was better than having to fight yourself out of a mess.

Rising, Troy said, "We should get over to the hotel to see how much we can help Bill and Frances. They probably have gotten enough extra gifts from the relatives in Albuquerque that they will need us. Don, if you and Aubrey will take the wagon over there, I will get my horse and meet you there."

"We will do it, Troy. Can you think of anything we need to take other than the wagon?"

"No, that should be enough for now, especially since we are likely bringing the wagon back to camp for the night anyway. Well, I will get Brindle saddled and see you out back of the hotel."

"Ok, Troy, we will see you there in about an hour."

Don and Aubrey had the wagon ready to go, except for hitching up the horses. They had previously had four mules hitched to the wagon as they drove it over the long trail from St. Louis, but the mules had been sold in Santa Fe. Now, they had four sturdy horses to do the pulling. That should be adequate to get the wagon to Chihuahua. Bill and Frances's load should not be as heavy as the load of commercial goods brought from St. Louis to Santa Fe.

Troy stopped to see Joseph Gonzales, the local blacksmith, about Brindle's gate. There seemed to be something wrong with the way he was moving today. He had never noticed the problem before, so was hoping it was minor.

Joseph was working with metal that he had stacked in front of the shop when Troy rode up.

"Joseph, how are you?"

He turned toward Troy with a smile on his face. "Fine, Troy. How are you?"

"I am fine; but Brindle is walking strangely this morning. Could you look at him?"

"I certainly can. Do you know which foot is bothering him?

As Troy finished dismounting, he said, "It feels like the left front, but I'm not entirely certain."

Joseph took Brindle's bridle and tied him to a metal ring at the front door of his shop. Then he gently patted and rubbed him while walking around looking at his legs and feet. He finally stopped by the right front leg and rubbed his hands down the leg and then back up.

Brindle seemed relaxed, so Joseph bent over and picked up the foot. After looking at it carefully, he said, "Troy, I think I have found your problem. And I think I can tell where you have been."

Taking a knife out of his pocket and digging into the bottom of the foot, he soon extracted a small lava rock and presented it to Troy.

Troy looked at the rock and said, "Yes, I bet you can tell where I have been or at least close. I was out close to the area where all the petroglyphs are, but not really in it yet."

"There are these smaller rocks all over that area. You do not need to get close to the big rocks to pick up these smaller ones. And once a rock gets stuck in a hoof, it wants to stay longer than smoother stones. When that volcano blew up, it must have been an enormous explosion. You would not believe how far from here I have seen collections of that lava rock. Of course, a lot of the lava must have flowed for miles. Now, it is weathered down to, little rocks in most places, except for the petroglyphs our ancestors decorated."

"That is fascinating. My brothers and I are planning to go see that area in a day or so. Say, speaking of brothers, my three brothers are probably waiting for me to help load some things in the wagon that will need to go to Chihuahua. I had better go. Thank you for your help."

"You are welcome, Troy. I hope to see you again soon."

Just as Troy was about to mount Brindle, a bay horse and rider came by the blacksmith shop at a full gallop. He had not even slowed down as he hit the edge of town. Troy turned to Joseph and asked, "Who was that? I wonder why he was in such a hurry?"

"That is Thomas Trask, Troy. I had hoped he was gone for good. As far as I can remember, it has been six months since I saw him last. All he wants to do is fight and act like a bigshot. I really think he is some kind of thief. It seems like things start disappearing when he hits town. I suggest you try to avoid him."

"I certainly will, Joseph. Thanks for the warning."

When Troy got to the hotel, Don, and Aubrey were already loading a small table into the wagon. There were several other items by the wagon, but not too many. With Troy's help, they had the load finished in a few minutes.

Don and Aubrey put a tarp over the wagon and were about to take the wagon back to camp when Bill and Frances came out of the hotel. "Hey, we would be happy to buy you lunch. Whatever they are cooking inside sure smells good."

Troy said, "We certainly have not done much work, but we will take you up on your offer anyway."

As they were heading into the hotel, Aubrey asked, "Troy, what took you so long to get here? I thought you would beat us here."

"I stopped to get Joseph at the blacksmith shop to look at Brindle's feet. He was favoring one of them. Joseph found a small lava rock that was wedged in tight."

"I didn't think you had been out there yet," said Don.

"Don, I did not think I had been there either. I knew we were close, but not to the site yet. However, the area with some lava stretches for miles, according to Joseph. While we have that place on our minds, I think we should go out there. We should go tomorrow, after we see Bill, Frances, and her family off to Chihuahua."

Aubrey said, "Sounds good to me, Troy."

"Me too, Troy," Don added.

Lunch came quickly after they all sat down in the hotel dining room. It smelled good because it was good. There were potatoes, onions, peppers, and parsnips all covered with a white cream gravy. Small bits of chicken were also in the gravy.

"Bill, tell us about your first trip between here and Chihuahua," said Troy. "Can you describe the countryside?"

Bill took a deep breath and said, "It is beautiful most of the way to Chihuahua. Even the area where we had the battle is attractive. We were just there at the wrong time. There were some young braves out just trying to make trouble. They stumbled across us and thought we were alone, so they attacked. If they had been there thirty minutes earlier, they would have seen our caravan. That probably would have caused them to leave and not come back.

"But they did attack, and it cost the lives of two good men and several of their braves. And it almost cost me my life too. Thank goodness, Carlos was with us. He is a merchant in Santa Fe that had originally been a soldier in the Spanish Army. They had trained him to treat all kinds of injuries for his fellow soldiers and that is why he was able to save my life. He got the wounds clean and kept them that way until I healed. After three weeks or so I was good as new. Oh, I felt terrible for a while, but Carlos gave me the confidence to think I was going to eventually be well. And sure enough, I was.

"I healed about the time we got to Chihuahua, and I met Frances," Bill said as he smiled at Frances.

Frances said, "I had no idea how badly he had been injured on the trip until later when someone at a family gathering was telling about the fight with a dozen Indians. They said that two men from here in Albuquerque were killed and Bill came close to being killed. By that time, Bill and I already knew each other well and he had not said anything about it."

"Oh, I just didn't want to tell her the gruesome details, so I didn't say anything," Bill followed up.

Troy said, "Bill, I am sure glad you made it. With you being injured so badly I am surprised that you remembered the rest of the trip."

"Troy, there was a week or ten days that I was laying in the wagon not knowing anything much. But then I started to get my strength back and started setting up with the driver. But remember, I did come back that same way returning to Santa Fe, so the route is not unfamiliar to me. From Albuquerque to Chihuahua, the entire way is dry and rugged, not desolate. The countryside is quite beautiful. Most of the trail is along the Rio Grande River as it cuts its way through hills and mountains. Then eventually you split from the river and go more directly south. There is one extremely sandy desert area before you are finished with the river. However, during that part of the route, the river does swing away from you. At that point you need to carry plenty of water for you and your horses.

"At some point before you leave the river for good, the vegetation changes and you will see desert plants you have never seen before. I think it is fascinating. I hope you will too. All together the trail from Albuquerque is about 450 miles, so it will take some time; but the trip is enjoyable."

"I am looking forward to the trip, Bill. With you and your group leaving in the morning, Don, Aubrey, and I should be about ten days or so behind you.

"I bet you and Frances are looking forward to getting back to Chihuahua and starting your new lives together."

"We certainly are," Frances and Bill said together, as they sat there holding hands.

Bill added, "I think for a while we will live in the house in town as Claudio and I work at building another house at the ranch. We will probably start by building one large room that we can use as a bedroom, kitchen and living room all together. Later, we will divide that room into a kitchen and living room; but not until we have built on a couple of bedrooms. Then, we will expand from there."

"What time will you be leaving in the morning?" Aubrey asked.

"My parents want to leave shortly after the sun is up," Frances answered.

"Ok," Troy said, "We will get here about that time to see you off. For now, I have a couple of people to see before the day is over. See you all in the morning."

"See you then," Bill said.

Don and Aubrey got in the wagon and headed back to camp, with a stop or two along the way. They wanted to buy a few supplies for cooking. Their flour was getting low, so they needed that along with salt, pepper, and a little tin of cooking grease.

Troy headed out on his errands. His first stop was to see Theo Fuentes, who was a builder. He and Troy had been talking about Theo building a store for Troy, that would be ready when he came back from New Orleans.

After a great deal of thinking, he was certain that he wanted to move his operation to Albuquerque. He intended to sell his store in New Orleans to his partners, along with all the merchandise they wanted to keep. Then he would buy enough wagons and hire enough men to move the remaining merchandise to Albuquerque.

It was his intention to let Don and Aubrey do whatever they wanted concerning the move.

The three of them were going to Chihuahua to see Bill, Frances, and her family. Then they would find a ship and sale across the Gulf of Mexico to New Orleans. From there, Don and Aubrey could go back to Alabama to farm again. Or they could stay in New Orleans and find work there. Troy's hope was that they would return to Albuquerque with him and either work for him or someone else. He wanted them to do what they wanted to do. It was nice to have family close by, so working in Albuquerque was his hope.

Troy found Theo inside his shop, at his work table. "Hi, Theo. How are you today?"

"Great, Troy. How are you?"

"I am almost great myself, Theo. I would be better, If I was not thinking about our trips to Chihuahua and New Orleans."

"Oh, Troy, the trip from here to Chihuahua should not be hard. The road has been quiet lately, because of Mexican soldiers patrolling the trail. And if you take my advice and sail across the Gulf, that part of the trip should not be difficult. You can just set back and let the ship do all the work. And it will save you lots of time."

"Theo, you have me convinced. Sailing is the way to go. In my younger days, I did some sailing on a couple of cargo ships up and down the coast from New Orleans to Boston. I would not mind having a taste of that life again. And sailing across the Gulf of Mexico should not be too tough unless we run into storms."

"Yes, you had better look out. You may enjoy it so much that you decide to start the sailing-life over. Then we will never see you again."

"No, Theo. I would never do that again for full time work. It certainly gets old after a while, sailing up and down the coast. I loved it for a while, but when it was over, it was over. I look forward to one short safe trip."

"I think that is what you will have, Troy."

"What did you think of those plans I left with you?" Troy asked. "Is that something you could work up for me before I get back next summer?"

"Yeah, I think I could handle that, especially if you can get me enough money to get started."

"That should not be a problem. I talked to Landis at the bank. He said that he has a relationship with a bank in New Orleans that can transfer money to him per my request. I will get in touch with the bank and get that underway."

"Sounds good, Troy. I certainly hope you and your brothers have a quick and safe trip back to New Orleans. And of course, back here also. A ship certainly is the way to go. It is not close enough to storm season that you should have any problems with bad weather.

Pirates are also a possibility. Whichever way you go will have its challenges. The nice thing about traveling by ship is how fast and direct it is."

"Theo, did you ever sail? It is quite the adventure. I sailed with Frances' cousin, Juan. We had a great time together and learned a lot about sailing. After about a year, we both decided to quit and go back home. I did not go home to Alabama. I stopped in New Orleans. Juan went back to Santa Fe and then finally settled down between Santa Fe and Taos. He built a trading post there. I guess both of us got the trading bug from being on those merchant ships. We will certainly keep an eye out for weather and pirates. I look forward to seeing how it feels to be on a ship again. I remember when I sailed the first time. I didn't really get my sea legs for almost a week. I felt terrible until then. After that, it was only in stormy weather that I felt sick."

Theo said, "I did sail for a season when I was about twenty. I loved it once I got my sea legs. The ship was constantly moving and could certainly make good time. We sailed mainly from Matamoros to the tip of the Yucatan and back again. It was great fun. I would not have quit when I did but my father was needing help on several of his building projects. I came home to Albuquerque and probably will never leave again. But it is nice to have those sailing memories. Speaking of that, when you get back from New Orleans, I will expect a full description of your trip."

Troy said, "My friend, you will certainly have a full description as soon as I get home to Albuquerque. Of course, it may not all be entirely true. You know us sailors. But it will be somewhere near the truth, I am certain."

Theo laughed loudly and then said, "I bet it will be close enough to the truth for me."

After visiting with Theo, Troy stopped by to see Justine to see how she was doing. The day was hot, so she had all the windows and doors open to allow any breeze to flow through.

"Hi, Troy. How are you doing? Bill and Frances and her parents are leaving in the morning, aren't they?"

"Yes, Bill said they would be leaving about the time the sun comes up. Aubrey, Don, and I are going to see them off. We are going to keep one of their wagons and take it to them in a week or so when we head that way. I thought we would stay here another ten days, but I think we will leave earlier than that. The more I think about the trip to New Orleans, the farther away it sounds. And the longer we stay here or Chihuahua, the more likely we are to find ourselves in storm season when we get on a ship. And, speaking of ships, we have no idea what their schedules are. We will just have to get to the port and wait for one going the right direction."

"Troy, I have enjoyed getting to know you and will be looking forward to your return. If there is some way I can help you, just let me know. And if I cannot help you, one of my family members might be able to."

"I might take you up on that someday. Theo is going to build a building for me that I can use to operate a store out of when I get back. When we or I get back, I know there will be lots of work to do."

"Are your brothers coming back with you?"

"Justine, I don't really know. I want them to, but I am almost afraid to ask them for fear they will want to return home and start farming again. At some point, I will sit down with them and see what they are thinking. Up till now I have been assuming they will come back and hoping they will come back. But, yeah, I don't really know."

"I will pray for you and them, that everything turns out ok, whatever you all decide."

"Thank you, Justine. I would really appreciate your prayers, especially for good decisions on everybody's part and for a safe trip."

Justine reached across the counter and took Troy's hand. She gave it a firm squeeze and said, "I'll see you in the morning to see everybody off on their trip to Chihuahua."

4 | VOLCANO

The next morning just as the sun was starting to glow below the eastern horizon, Troy, Aubrey, and Don arrived at the hotel. Bill, Frances, and her family were already there preparing to leave for Chihuahua. Justine arrived a few minutes after the Rampy brothers.

Frances was rearranging a few things in their wagon as Bill and Claudio were loading the last of the luggage. She turned around and spoke to the brothers. "Good morning. How are you all this morning? I bet you wish you were going with us, instead of staying here another two weeks." She laughed, meaning the comment to be a joke; but that was exactly what the guys were feeling. All three of them were anxious to get back on the trail to Chihuahua and then on to New Orleans.

Don said, "Well, we do have a few important things planned before we can slip away. If it was not for that, I am sure we would love to go right now."

"Don's right," said Aubrey. "We honestly do have a few things planned, but it would be nice to go with you."

There were two wagons and six horses lined up in front of

the hotel. They would carry Bill, Frances, and Frances' family and several friends that had originally come along to Santa Fe for Ronaldo's ceremony and then accidentally for Bill and Frances' wedding.

The hotel had prepared an earlier than normal breakfast for the travelers. They were all filled and ready to head south now. While Justine was saying goodbye to Frances' parents and sister, Bill and Frances were saying goodbye to his brothers. Dolores had also come out of the hotel kitchen and was saying goodbye to everyone, along with Jesse and Aunt Fiona, who had just arrived.

Finally, Claudio cleared his throat, and said, "We need to get on the road before lunch, so let's mount up."

Everyone did as Claudio suggested, and their caravan started rolling south. Troy told Bill they would be heading that way sooner than he intended. He was getting anxious to get on the road, so hopefully they would be leaving Albuquerque in a week or less.

As the caravan got well down the road, Troy and the guys decided to go into the hotel to see if Dolores had some breakfast left. Aunt Fiona and Jesse had already eaten, so they headed home. Troy asked Justine if he could buy her breakfast. She smiled and accepted the offer.

As it turned out, Dolores had plenty of breakfast left. Over a pot of coffee and a full breakfast, they discussed plans for the week ahead. Today, Troy and his brothers would go exploring in the lava bed to see the petroglyphs. Justine was going to have her store open as normal. Then later in the week, she would be sorting some new inventory.

"What will you guys do for the rest of the week?" Justine asked. "I could use some help cleaning out the back of my store," she said with a laugh.

Aubrey said, "I think you could talk Troy into that, if you talked hard enough. Or I suppose you could talk us into it also.

I am not sure what Don and I will be doing for the rest of the week. Troy is really the only one of us that has plans. Well, other than seeing the lava beds and generally exploring the area."

"It is settled then. As soon as you run out of anything to do, come over to my store and I will put you to work. And I probably will even feed you."

"Sounds good to us," said Don.

The four of them sat for a long time, until Justine said, "I am late opening my store. I had better get over there. You guys have a pleasant day viewing the petroglyphs. Watch out for the rattlesnakes."

Troy and his brothers dismounted, and ground tied their horses when they got to the edge of the decorated volcanic stones. They had never seen anything like it before. According to Jesse, nobody knew when or why the rocks were decorated.

The designs on the rocks were apparently etched onto the stones by natives of the area hundreds or maybe thousands of years earlier. Nobody knew if this was just art or if the symbols were religious in some way. There were symbols of people, animals, birds, landscapes and even things that looked like objects flying in the air. Some of the designs were not understandable at all, yet they were all interesting.

It was a fascinating area to explore, although you did have to keep an eye out for snakes. Just as Justine and Jesse warned, the area did have more than its fair share of large, deadly rattlesnakes.

After the guys had their fill of the rocks, they rode up into the foothills nearby and looked back toward town. Albuquerque looked larger from the hilltop than it did down on the ground. It was a beautiful sight looking down at the river and across it to the town. Troy felt even more confident in his decision to sell his store in New Orleans and move his entire operation to Albuquerque.

Troy and his brothers spent the rest of the day roaming around the countryside just to enjoy the beauty of the area. Later, at their campsite, there was plenty to talk about from the day's activities to what the future looked like for each of them.

"I am worn out," said Troy. "That was quite a day. I think my favorite thing was riding up into the hills and enjoying the views. It was spectacular enough to take your breath away.

"What did you guys like most?"

Don said, "I agree with the hills and the beauty of the area. I have a real soft spot in my heart for things that happened long ago, like the lava beds and those petroglyphs. You cannot beat the scenery of this area. Spectacular is certainly the right word for it. I hear that the big mountains to the west and farther north are unbelievable, so I would like to see them someday. For right now though, I think today's scenery is the most spectacular thing I have ever seen.

"Aubrey, what was your favorite thing today?"

"I grant you the scenery is spectacular," said Aubrey. "I loved it; but the thought of ancient people decorating rocks hundreds or thousands of years ago was unbelievable to me. I was over-whelmed by that."

"Yes, it was a special day," said Troy. "I enjoyed it a great deal."

After a pause, Troy said, "Guys, I have been meaning to talk to you about your intentions for the future. We have been on our current adventure for some time. You both seemed to have been willing participants on the trip. And I have not heard you talking about going home to Alabama to continue farming. Before I ask you about your intentions, it is only fair that I tell you mine."

He took a breath and continued. "I originally thought I would come out here and start a second store in Santa Fe or Albuquer-que, if it seemed like a good decision once I got here. I would keep the store in New Orleans as the main store. I thought if either or both of you were interested in staying with me, you could work for me or partner with me in either store. However, now I am thinking I will sell my interest in the New Orleans store to my partners and have only one store here in Albuquerque. If either of you wants to work in New Orleans instead of coming back here, I am sure that my partners could put you to work. Of course, I realize that you may want to go home and continue farming."

"So, with all that said, what are you both thinking about the future? Let me say, too, that I have immensely enjoyed working with you these past few months. I would like to continue that. It is your choice to make."

"Troy, when Don and I originally left Alabama and headed to New Orleans to see you and Bill, I had no intentions of leaving home or farming for good. Now, I cannot imagine going back to that life. And to be completely honest, I am not entirely certain I want to live the rest of my life here in Albuquerque. However, that is certainly an option.

"Living in New Orleans would also be an option. Until you decided to make Albuquerque the center of your operation, I assumed I would work with you in New Orleans and make that my home. Now, I am not sure what I want to do. I will have to give that some thought.

"Farming was hard, yet rewarding. I thought I would do that forever. It was lonely in a way. Even with lots of family around, it seemed like something was missing. We were so far from town that we rarely saw anybody that was not family. Now, having some exposure to larger towns, I know that is more comfortable in many ways. Who knows? Maybe I could find a wife someday if I stay in town."

All three laughed at that.

"What are you thinking, Don," Troy asked?

Don laughed again and said, "I agree completely with Aubrey, especially about finding a wife. I was beginning to feel like the two of us would remain bachelors forever. And that would not be because we wanted to, but because there were just no prospects in those Alabama hills.

"I also agree when it comes to where I want to live. I certainly liked New Orleans, but Albuquerque is growing on me too. And, frankly, working with you two has been great. I am not sure I want to live anywhere that the two of you don't live.

"Troy, with you wanting to build your business here, I think I would intend to make a home here also."

"Wow," Aubrey said, "That feels like pressure for me to stay here." He laughed. "I would still like to see New Orleans again, before I make up my mind completely. However, the idea of living near you two does sound appealing."

"I am glad to hear all that, guys," Troy said, "because I would also like for us to be near each other. With Bill just six hundred or so miles south of here, hopefully, we would see him and Frances from time to time also.

"We can get things wrapped up here in a few days. After that, we should go to Chihuahua, see Bill and on to the Gulf Coast to find a ship heading to New Orleans."

"Sounds good," Aubrey and Don both said.

5 | TROUBLE IN TOWN

The next morning Troy headed into town to talk to a couple of additional business people he had not met.

Aubrey and Don got things buttoned up at the campsite and went to the hotel to eat breakfast. It seemed to them that the other people eating in the hotel were especially quiet. It was not clear why. After breakfast they headed to Justine's shop to see if they could help her.

As the three of them headed out, none of them realized how this day would impact their lives forever.

When Justine saw the guys come into her shop, she got a big smile on her face and said, "Well, if it is not the Rampy clan. What are you guys up to today?"

Aubrey said, "We came to help you, like we promised the other day. Where can we start?"

Justine laughed and said, "I was only joking. I am not sure what I need help with."

"We are free labor." Aubrey added, "So surely you can find something for us to do. We work inside or outside and are generally experienced in a wide variety of tasks."

They both chuckled at that.

"Ok, guys, let me see what I can find for you to do." She took a tablet and headed into the back room.

Fifteen minutes later, she had a long list of things that needed doing. First the guys worked on inventorying a quantity of smaller items. Then they inventoried larger items. Next came organizing shelves.

Around noon, Justine ran over to the hotel and brought back some large sandwiches.

It had been a busy morning in the store, so Justine had left Don and Aubrey alone while they worked. Now, she took the sandwiches to the back and was surprised by how much work they had done. "Wow, you guys have been busy. Thank you so much. I really do not know what to say. You are great!"

"We wanted to give you your money's worth," said Aubrey. He and Don chuckled. "So, you think our work was ok?"

"I brought you a little food for lunch. I don't think it is nearly enough."

"That is more than enough," said Don, who was already starting on one of the sandwiches.

"You guys have finished more than half the list I gave you. That is amazing."

"I guess that means we should take the rest of the day off. Then we can come back tomorrow," suggested Don.

Aubrey said, "That sounds good to me."

"Oh, guys, that is much too generous. What you have done is more than I ever could have expected from anybody, even if I was paying them."

"Rampys are funny that way," said Don. "We will do almost anything for a free meal."

Justine laughed and said, "I will keep that in mind."

The three of them sat and ate. The guys talked about growing up in Alabama and their family there. Their farming was also something they talked about. Justine talked about growing up in

Albuquerque, her relatives, her marriage, her daughter, and the years she had spent in the store.

Justine's store was getting busy again, so the guys said they would be back the next day and left.

About mid-afternoon Thomas Trask came into the store with all his swagger. Fortunately, Justine continued to be busy. Trask finally came to the counter with one small item he bought. Then he left.

Justine, who had known of Trask and his dark reputation the last time he was in town, was shaken by his appearance in her store. She was still emotionally rocky when Troy came by a little before her normal closing time.

Troy came in with a smile on his face. It changed slightly when he saw Justine. He said, "Justine, are you alright? You look like you are in pain."

"Oh, Troy, Thomas Trask came into the store. He just scares me. This town has always been my home and I always feel safe here, except when he is around. The last time he was here there were several robberies and a couple of shootings. I made the mistake of walking past the front door of the saloon one afternoon. He came out and grabbed me and tried to kiss me. I fought him off and got out of there quickly. Now, every time I see him, I feel like he is going to grab me again. He is just such an evil person."

"I do not know if it will help you feel better but you should close your store for the day. Then you and Karina and I can go over to the hotel for supper. Hopefully, Dolores can fix something that will help you take your mind off that jerk."

"Troy, that would be nice of you. I can have this place closed in about three minutes. Then we can go by the house and get Karina."

Dolores was indeed able to fix a wonderful meal for the three of them while they sat and talked.

"Troy, you have great brothers. I have never seen two guys

work up such a storm as they did today. I did not think I needed any help. I could not believe what they had done by the time they took off for the day."

Troy said, "Thanks Justine. I am glad they were able to help. They will probably be back tomorrow because they do not have anything else to do before we head to Chihuahua. I do not have anything either, so all three of us might be there. But feel free to run us off if we are being pests."

"I will not run off workers like you guys. Surely, I can find some way to keep you busy.

Justine added, "Say, did you hear anything about the shooting earlier today? I talked to a couple of people who came into the shop except they did not know who had been shot."

Troy said, "I heard that Chico Monera was shot and killed. Apparently, nobody saw it happen. Chico was shot in the chest, so they thought it was a gun fight and not a murder. He had been at the bar earlier, so must have rubbed somebody the wrong way. It is still too bad. This country is getting rougher as the population grows."

Justine said, "That is for certain. It makes me sad."

"Me too, Justine. Me too. I will walk you ladies, home. I need to get back to our camp and get some sleep. Sounds like we will have a hard day tomorrow."

It was a pleasant walk to Justine's and then out to their camp. Aubrey and Don were sitting by a small fire talking. Don said, "Troy, where have you been? We did not know you had evening plans."

"Oh, I stopped by Justine's store, and she was sort of shook up. The local jerk Tomas Trask came into her store when she was busy. He left before she had to talk to him. She apparently had a run-in with him the last time he was in town. Now she is afraid of him. Or maybe disgusted by him, would be more accurate."

"Trask, I heard his name earlier in the day," said Don. "The rumor floating around town is that Trask is likely responsible for the shooting early this morning. Some folks were saying that the death looked like a gun fight, but most do not believe that. They say that Trask probably was waiting for him and shot him without warning. Of course, nobody knows for sure."

Troy said, "I hate that we are leaving so soon, considering how Justine feels about Trask. She needs somebody around to protect her. The entire town knows and loves her and her daughter, but that can only go so far toward protecting her. I had been thinking about leaving for Chihuahua the day after tomorrow. Now I am thinking we might wait a while longer."

"Sounds good to me," said Aubrey.

"Me too," said Don. "We can stay as long as you think we should."

"But the good news," said Troy, "is that Justine was amazed by your work today and she has invited all of us back for tomorrow. She is making a whole new list."

"Great," said Don. Then they all laughed. There was a feeling amongst all of them that tomorrow might be more exciting than they wanted it to be.

The next morning before sunrise, they were all up and drinking coffee around the fire. Aubrey had broken out some of the beef jerky that was left over from their original load-out in New Orleans. "Wow, now this is some tough chewing. When was this made?"

Don said, "I think I bought two cases of that at Troy's store in New Orleans. I cannot believe that we still have some of it."

"It is slow chewing. I suppose that is why it has lasted so long. Troy, would you like some aged jerky?"

Troy laughed and said, "No, I do not think so. I would like to keep my teeth for a while longer. Thanks for the thought anyway. Are you guys excited to go see Justine and her new list?"

Aubrey said with a laugh, "I thought we fixed everything in her store yesterday. You mean we missed something?"

"Apparently so. She said she would make a new list for today. Of course, she may have been kidding me. Let's go by and see."

When they reached the store, Troy's guess proved to be accurate.

Justine said, "Good morning, gentlemen. I am surprised you came back after how hard you worked yesterday." Then with a laugh she said, "Would you like some hot coffee and cinnamon rolls?"

Don offered, "I think we could handle that. I cannot believe that we did everything you needed to do yesterday."

Justine laughed. Then she said, "You know there are a few things we could all do together, it you are still up to it, after the coffee."

As it turned out, they spent most of the morning rearranging the front of the store. Don and Aubrey moved the counters around per Justine's direction. Then Troy and Justine rearranged the stock.

"Justine, that was fun," said Troy. "I have not worked on stock since we left my store several months ago. I forgot how satisfying it is to arrange displays that you feel will catch a customer's eye."

"Troy, I am glad you enjoyed it. Now, I should buy us all lunch. Then you guys can take the rest of the day off."

That got a laugh from the guys. The four of them had lunch. Justine went back to the shop and the guys all had separate errands they wanted to finish before they left for Chihuahua.

The afternoon had gone well for Justine. With more than the normal number of visitors in her store the day seemed to go quickly. Then toward the end of the business day it got especially quiet. The weather outside was looking stormy and had driven people to seek shelter.

As she was starting to close the store, she had one last customer come in. It was Thomas Trask.

"Ms. Martinez, how are you? It has been a long time."

"I am fine, thanks, Mr. Trask. How can I help you? I am closing-up for the day."

"Oh, I just wanted to see you and ask how you are doing." He walked slowly toward the counter.

Justine was beginning to feel threatened as he moved closer to the counter. He moved toward the end of the counter that blocked her way to get out from behind the counter. Now her only way to the front door was to jump on the counter and slide across. She was wearing a skirt, so that seemed like a poor option.

"How can I help you, Mr. Trask? I really need to close the store and take care of some other business."

He slipped around behind the counter and walked slowly toward her. "Oh, taking care of business was what I had in mind. As you probably recall, I kissed you once and I just wanted to do it again."

He was almost in reach of her now. She thought the only option she had was to run out the back door. As she turned to run through the door behind the counter, he grabbed her by the shoulder and pushed her into the back room.

Troy finished his visits around town and was headed toward Justine's store when he ran into his brothers.

"Hi Troy. Don and I were discussing going to the hotel for supper, since we are leaving in the morning. Do you want to join us?"

"Sounds like a good idea. You guys go on to the hotel and I'll stop by Justine's store to see if she is still there."

As Troy approached the store, he thought it was closed because there was no light inside. Thankfully, he tried the front door and found it unlocked. Just then, he heard a scream.

Rushing into the store and then into the back room, he found Justine wrestling to get loose from Thomas Trask's grip. He had torn her dress. It was completely off her right shoulder and down her back.

It took Troy about four large steps to get to Trask. By that time, Trask saw Troy. He pushed Justine away and pulled his gun. Troy hit the gun as it was coming up causing it to fire and fell from Trask's hand. The sound echoed through the small room.

Troy pushed Trask back against the wall. Then with his right hand, he was able to get one good punch to Trask's head.

Trask fell to the side and recovered quickly. He ran at Troy like a bull and knocked him to the ground. Troy's pistol fell from his holster and slid across the floor. Trask got in two punches to Troy's head before Troy pushed him off and rolled to the side.

Troy was able to get up and charge at Trask. Trask pushed a wooden crate in his path and then threw a smaller box at Troy's head.

Troy threw up his arm to fend off the box. The edge of it hit his head, stunning him momentarily. Trask ran at Troy again and knocked him down.

As Trask lunged at him again, Troy rolled to the side and got to his feet.

As Troy moved toward Trask, Trask drew a knife he had strapped to his leg. He charged toward Troy. Troy side-stepped him and grabbed a wooden lath.

The lath was no match for the long-bladed knife, but it did cause Trask to stop momentarily to think about his next move.

Just then, a loud bang rang through the room. Trask's body jerked violently, and he fell to the floor.

Troy looked in the direction of the noise and saw Justine standing where she had retrieved his pistol. She was shaking so badly that she could barely stand. Tears were rolling down her cheeks.

The two of them stood in stunned silence for a few seconds. Then Troy walked over to her and put his arms around her. She stood shaking and then finally laid her cheek against his. She said, "Oh, Troy, I was so scared. I did not know what to do, except fight and hope he did not kill me."

"I am thankful that I stopped by the store when I did. I heard you scream as I was trying the front door." Troy was shaking now in rhythm with Justine's shaking. They stood there and held each other until they heard noise in the store.

At that time, Aubrey, Don, and another man rushed into the back room. Each man had his pistol drawn. They had shocked looks on their faces when they saw Justine's dress and Trask's body on the floor.

The three men had been standing in front of the hotel when they heard the first pistol shot. They could not tell where it came from. When they heard the second gun shot, they could tell it was coming from the store.

"Are you two alright," Don asked softly?

"Yes, I think we are now. Justine just saved my life," said Troy.

"And Troy just saved my life," Justine said, while still shaking.

Troy finally let Justine go and said, "I guess we should go talk to the Justice of the Peace. And maybe the barber can come get the body and bury him. I do not know if Trask had any friends here, so a funeral service will probably not be necessary."

Justine found a jacket under her counter to cover the damage to her dress. Then they walked to the house of the Justice of the Peace and told him the story of the attack.

After listening to the story told by his cousin Justine, the Justice of the Peace said, "Justine, I am awfully sorry this happened to you and thank goodness that Mr. Rampy showed up when he did. I will talk to Juan about the body and get it moved out of your store. He can bury him on the back side of the cemetery. There is a spot there for unidentified bodies. Although, if he has some money in his pocket, we could get somebody to make a simple headstone for him."

"Will there need to be a trial?" Justine asked timidly.

"No, everybody around town knows Mr. Trask's reputation. They will all be glad to know he is gone. Nobody in Albuquerque would doubt the truth of your story."

The four of them walked back to the store. Justine locked up once Juan got the body out of the back room. None of them felt like supper now. They went to Justine's house. She made a pot of coffee and they talked. Fortunately, Karina was spending the night with Aunt Fiona. Justine would have lots of explaining to do in the morning.

Justine quit crying after the sixth or so time. She said, "I do not know why I keep crying. I am not sure if it was because I was so afraid of Trask, or if I was scared that he was going to kill you, Troy, or if it was because I killed a man. I suppose it must be a bit of all three. It just makes me want to shake all over. I am not sure I will be able to keep the store open by myself. Every time the door opens, I will startle. And if a stranger comes in, I will probably start crying again. It does not sound like a good way to run a business."

Troy said, "You have quite a few relatives around town. Maybe, you can get some of them to come in and set with you at the store until you feel comfortable again. And, if you would like, Aubrey, Don and I could wait a few days or a week before we leave for Chihuahua. Of course, you will need to make another list of projects for us to work on." They all laughed.

"I like that idea a lot. If you men could stay around for another week, it would make me feel better."

"We would be glad to do that," said Troy.

"I don't really want to stay by myself tonight and since Karina is at Aunt Fiona's house, I think I will go sleep on her couch. Karina should be asleep by now, so I will not have to explain anything to her until morning.

Would you gentlemen walk with me over there?"

The four of them walked to Aunt Fiona's, where they found Fiona awake. She came out on the front porch to hear Justine's story. The story made her cry, which made Justine start to cry again. Once they were both feeling a little calmer, the guys told Justine they would see her in the morning and headed back to camp.

6 | LEAVING ALBUQUERQUE

The next morning, Troy and his brothers got up a little late and went to the hotel for breakfast. Justine told them before they left Fiona's that she probably would not try to open until mid-morning. After they finished their second or third cup of coffee, they walked over to Justine's store.

Justine was just getting there when they arrived. She said, "I am glad you guys are here. I have been shaking, just thinking about opening the store. Hopefully, I will be better now. Troy, how are you? I have been so concerned about myself that I did not think about you and how you would be feeling. That was some fight you had with Trask. You must feel like a horse ran over you."

"I feel better just to know that you are alright. Oh, I am sore but glad to have survived. Trask was even stronger than I thought he might be. Without you being there, he might have gotten the advantage once he pulled out that knife."

"Oh, Troy, I am glad we were there for each other." Justine started to cry and then stopped herself. "I have got to quit doing that. Besides, I have a list to make for you guys." She laughed and the guys smiled at each other.

While Justine got the front of the store ready for the day, the guys went to the back of the store to clean up any evidence of last night's fight. The rest of the day was business as usual for Justine. It did not take her long to get settled down and feeling more comfortable. The guys stayed around the store and did whatever they could to help.

Toward the end of the day, Troy was helping Justine in the front of the store. As one remaining customer left the store, Troy said, "Justine, you seem to be feeling better. How has the day gone for you?"

She smiled and said, "Good. I think I am feeling almost back to normal. How are you feeling?"

"I am still sore, and probably will be for another day or so. The exertion you use in a fight like that must use more than your normal muscles, so it leaves you far sorer than you would expect."

"Troy, I feel like I am going to be fine around the store now. I have had so many sympathetic friends and family come by the store today. It has cheered me up more than I would have imagined. If you, Aubrey, and Don want to leave, I am sure I will be alright."

"I think we will stay another couple of days. After that, we will head south. I am anxious to see Chihuahua. Bill and Frances told us a lot about it. It sounds like a nice place for them to make a life together."

"It certainly will," Justine said. "And with Frances' family there, it should be especially nice."

Troy said, "I do not remember if I have told you or not, but we intend to stay in Chihuahua for a couple of weeks. Then we will go to the Gulf Coast and hopefully find a ship sailing for New Orleans.

"When I was young, I originally left home and became a sailor on a commercial cargo ship. It sailed up and down the east coast of America. That is how I met your cousin Juan. Oh, maybe I have told you some of this story. Anyway, ever since my sailing days, I have wanted to be on a ship sailing across the gulf. I really am getting anxious to go. Although, I do not want to leave here too quickly, if there is any need for us to stay."

Justine walked up close to Troy and said, "I am not trying to run you off, but I can think of another reason for you to leave."

"And what would that be," he asked?

"Well, the quicker you leave, the faster you will be back. And I would not mind that." Then, she leaned in and kissed him firmly on the cheek.

Then Troy said, "Come to think of it, I would not mind that either."

They both laughed. Troy looked around to make sure there was nobody in the store. There was not, so he put his arms around her and kissed her gently on the lips. She returned the kiss.

Troy had not seen his brothers in the back of the store who were watching Troy and Justine up front. As brothers will, they had no intention of ever letting him forget that kiss.

Troy said, "I guess we will be leaving the day after tomorrow."

"Good," Justine said. "You three should come to my house and eat supper tonight. Karina and I would love to have you over."

"We will be there."

Supper at Justine's was simple and filling. Everyone seemed to be more interested in talking than eating. Troy gave Justine more information about their coming trip to Chihuahua, and on to New Orleans. At Justine's request, Don and Aubrey talked more about their childhood and early adult life in Alabama.

Don explained their farming, He said, "Aubrey and I farmed with our father when we were young. Then a neighbor asked us to farm for him. Then another neighbor lost his wife in a house fire just about the time he had put together a large farm. He asked us to farm it for him and moved back to Connecticut. We did farm it for two years and then he sold it to us. A portion of each crop would be his until we paid off the farm. The price for the farm was especially reasonable."

"Who is farming the land now?" Justine asked. "Did you sell it?"

"No, we had two good friends that wanted to farm it for us when we left to see Troy. They understood the arrangement we had with Mr. Hanson. They promised to be true to our agreement. Aubrey and I told them we would eventually be back even though we had no idea when. Of course, we had no idea it would take as-long-as it has. They probably think we have died."

Aubrey laughed and said, "They probably do think we have died. I am sure they will just keep farming the place until we get back. If we do get back."

"I probably should send them a letter, some day," Don said. They both laughed at that.

Troy asked Justine about their trips to Chihuahua when she was young. Justine said, "My family went to Chihuahua about every other year when I was growing up. There was always a large group of family and friends going at the same time. We went together partly for safety and partly for fun. It was a long trip, so it was nice to have everyone around to keep the trip from being boring. And there were lots of women to share the cooking. They would cook for the entire group, so we always had group meals. Breakfast and supper were the only meals. There were always tortillas, other breads, and dried meat when people needed something extra."

Troy asked, "What did the men do?"

She said, "A group of men would ride up front to show the way and another group bringing up the rear for protection and to pick up anything that was dropped. Safety was not as much of an issue then as it seems to be now. We saw Indians along the way, but they were all friendly. And there were no thieves along the trail, to speak of. Oh, I heard about a small robbery. but it was close to towns and not out in the middle of nowhere."

Aubrey asked, "How long did the trip usually take?

"The trip would take around three weeks, so it seemed like it was taking forever, especially to the children. Though, there were places that the children enjoyed. When we were near the river or certain hills that were fun to climb, the children had a great time. There was one set of hills that were always avoided because of a huge population of rattlesnakes. You guys will need to avoid it too. Remind me to draw you a map showing where the hills are along the trail. The hills are unusually rocky and obviously a perfect place for snakes. When we got to Chihuahua, it was wonderful. We got to see friends and family. There were dances, supper gatherings, and church services. Then we would come home again. I thought it was fantastic."

Don said with a chuckle, "I bet I would have loved that trip. It sounds like all the things I thought were fun was what you got to do.

Justine added, "One of those trips is how I met my husband, Radalfo. He was such a handsome man and could dance like a wildfire. We had several opportunities to dance and get to know each other. That year when we headed back to Albuquerque, Radalfo came with us. We got married when the trip was over. About a year later, we had Karina, the joy of our lives."

Troy said, "Bill told me that most of your family came here as immigrants from Spain. Was that before your time? Do you know anything about it?"

"Yes, our entire family came to Mexico as immigrants from Spain. It was long before my time. It is my understanding that Spain conquered the Aztec Empire and established New Spain. Then the King of Spain sent many ships loaded with immigrants here to settle this country for Spain. Before the Spanish settlers got here, the population was made up of different indigenous people groups. The last large group was the Aztecs. Of course, there were other smaller groups that were not Aztecs and some of them are still part of the population."

Justine added, "Now, the people of this country have finished a war with Spain and finally won their independence. I am proud to be from Spain and I am also proud to be a citizen of free Mexico. I think my family and friends all think the same way."

There were tears in Justine's eyes by the time she finished this story about her ancestors and the new country of Mexico.

"Our family were immigrants too," Troy said. "Our father was from Germany. He spoke German, as well Spanish and English. Our mother was from Spain. She spoke Spanish, French and English. We kids spoke a little of everything. There are us four boys. And we also have four sisters."

"What are your sister's names?" Justine asked.

"There is Jo Beth," said Troy. "She is the oldest. Then there is Onita, Willa, and Janette. They are back home with our parents. I suppose Jo Beth and Onita are probably married by now. They both had gentlemen friends, the last time I heard."

Aubrey said, "As far as we know, our mother and father are not in touch with any of their family back in their homelands. There are a few relatives that came to the United States also and they do exchange letters with them when they can. Do any of your family members communicate with family back in Spain?"

Justine said, "My parents are not living. When they were, there was some writing back and forth. The letters took months to get back and forth, so it was difficult. My father would write letters to his father and brother in Seville. Say, I think I promised you a map of the route from here to Chihuahua, or at least the rough spots along the way. I will get a sheet of paper and a pen and ink. I am not particularly artistic, so you will need to excuse my lack of talent."

Justine went to her bedroom for a few minutes. She had several pieces of paper and a bottle of ink and a quill pen when she returned.

She said, "I found a partial map. I was making it for someone else several years ago. They went with a group and did not need the map. Let me finish this map and then I will show you a few key points you will want to know."

She sat down by Troy and etched in a few places farther to the south than where the map had originally ended. "Of course, starting from Albuquerque you will follow the river. It apparently flows all the way to the Gulf of Mexico. You will turn off at this point where I drew a star. The town of Juarez is there. It is small. You can buy supplies if you are needing anything. The trail splits just west of town. Some people travel down the river, headed for Matamoros. Those going to Chihuahua will follow the trail directly south. The trail is traveled enough that it should be easy to follow.

Troy studied the map seriously. He knew that in an unknown area, one of your best tools was a good map and knowledge of how to read it.

Justine continued, "Now, let me start over again at Albuquerque and show you a few things. A day or so south of town I drew a small x. It is my understanding that is where Bill and part of his caravan were attacked by a group of about ten or twelve Indian braves. I think they were a hunting party made up of young braves who had more energy than good sense. The main part of the caravan had continued toward Chihuahua after lunch. Three wagons stayed back just long enough for a repair to one of the wagons. Just as they were ready to leave and rejoin the caravan, the Indians happened upon them. With the wagons looking like easy pickings, the Indians attacked. Two men in one wagon were killed almost instantly and Bill was seriously injured. Apparently before he went down, Bill killed one of the Indians. Several more were killed or seriously injured by the other men with the wagon. Then, the rest of the hunting party fled."

JIM EDD WARNER

"Yes, Bill told me most of that story," said Troy. "It sounded like almost an accident on the part of the hunting party. If the wagons had not looked, as you said, like easy pickings, the hunting party would not have attacked. As it was, they killed two men and almost killed Bill. Bill told me that he might not have made it except for the skill of a merchant from Santa Fe. His name was Carlos, I think. Bill said he had been in the Spanish Army and had learned a lot about treating wounds."

Justine smiled and said, "Yes, Carlos, another of my cousins. He comes to Albuquerque occasionally. I will have to introduce you some time. He learned more than medical treatment in the army and is a good person to have around."

Troy said, "Well, I am certainly glad he was around for Bill."

"The next obstacle," Justine continued, "is a large desert area they call Jornada del Muerto. At that point the river cuts through a rocky area that forces the trail to go through the sandy area. To cross the Jornada del Muerto will take you from two to three days. There is no water, so you will need to carry water for yourself and your horses. If you were pulling heavy wagons full of goods, you would need to be careful to avoid the sandiest areas. They can almost swallow a wagon. Horses usually do not have a problem, but be careful anyway. "Pointing at another area on the map, she said, "This is the area where they have found the most snakes, so be especially careful around rocky hills."

"What is the area on the map that says hot springs?" asked Don.

"Oh, I have never been there, Don, but there is a path heading to the west just before you get to the Jornada del Muerto. It leads down into a canyon where there is a pool of hot water fed by a spring. I have heard many people speak fondly of it, but our family never stopped there. It seems slightly dangerous because if any robbers wanted to attack, that would be the best place. And I think it is a difficult place to get a wagon into and out of. So, I don't know enough to recommend it. If you try it, please be careful."

Don said, "Sounds interesting. If we try it, I will certainly remember your warning."

"Maybe we should head back to camp," Troy suggested, "so we can get an early start tomorrow. We can get everything wrapped up tomorrow and go see Bill and Frances the next day. Justine, is there anything we can help you with before we leave?"

"No, I am in pretty good shape. I would be glad to see you guys tomorrow. You could buy my lunch if you want to." They all laughed at that. Eating lunch together was becoming a habit for the four of them.

"Ok," Troy said, "We will see you sometime in the morning."

The guys headed back to camp and turned in for the night. Nights seemed to be getting shorter for some reason.

The next morning, they were up early taking care of the horses and making sure the wagon was buttoned down and ready to go. They had their own three horses and the four to pull the wagon. In addition, they had recently bought two more saddle horses. They would be tied to the back of the wagon on the trip and be used as spare saddle horses or for the wagon. On a five-hundred-mile journey, you can never tell what might happen to a horse. Or its rider, for that matter.

Lunch was had by the four together. They did not go to the restaurant. Justine brought it for them from home. After that the guys continued to work on a few items that needed to be finished. Then they headed back to camp to turn in early for the night.

Troy wanted them to move quickly on their trip to Chihuahua. He was hoping to make the normal twenty-to-thirty-day trip into a two-week trip.

7 | TO CHIHUAHUA

The three Rampys were up and ready to leave when the sun crept over the eastern horizon. Troy had made some coffee on the campfire. In addition, there was fresh bread Troy received the evening before as a gift from Justine.

"Troy, this coffee is not half bad," Aubrey said. "We should probably designate you as our camp cook on the way to Chihuahua."

"I would agree to that," Don said. "Besides, every family man should be able to cook."

"Well, I know you guys are family," Troy said, "but I do not know that cooking duties fall into the same category under this kind of situation. I do not think that I am exactly a family man."

"I am thinking you will be a family man as soon as you get back here from New Orleans." He laughed and added, "Aubrey and I saw you kiss Justine yesterday in the store. And that was no friendly peck on the cheek sort of kiss. It was more like a hi- sweetheart-I-am-home-from-work kind of kiss. You cannot deny that you and Justine have feelings for each other. I bet you

61

a hundred dollars that you and Justine will be married within a week after you return."

Even in the early morning light, it was still obvious that Troy had an embarrassed glow on his cheeks. He said, "Guys, I will not deny that I have feelings for Justine. I think she is the most special woman I have ever met, but I do not have any idea how she feels about me."

"She let you kiss her, didn't she?" asked Don.

"Guys, just because a woman lets you kiss her does not mean that she wants to marry you. And in this case, I really think she is still feeling emotionally close to me because of the incident with Trask. She took that all pretty hard. He scared her half to death. Then I show up and she thinks Trask is going to kill me. After that, she shoots Trask to save both of us. She felt awful about that. The idea of killing another human being is something she had never thought about until she was forced by circumstances to pull that trigger. We talked about the shot for a long time one night. Killing Trask was almost overwhelming to her. I told her that Trask deserved what he got. She agreed. but just wished it had not been her that did the shooting.

"With all that said, I still think that Justine feels close to me now, at least partially, because of the incident. I do not want to assume that she loves me when there are all those other possibilities hanging over the incident. Believe me, if Justine falls into my arms when I get back here from New Orleans, I would love it."

"And we wouldn't blame you a bit either," said Aubrey. "Oh, by the way, here she comes."

Troy jerked his head around and stood up from his log by the fire and said, "Good morning, Justine. How are you this morning?"

"I am not too good, considering that the man I love is going to the US and will not be back for several months. So, I am thinking that you three guys had better get out of here quick and get back quick. And keep yourselves safe and healthy along the way.

"Are you ready to go?"

"We are," said Troy.

"Ok, then give me a hug and get out of here."

Aubrey and Don, both gave her warm hugs. Then Troy put his arms around her softly and gave her a long kiss and warm embrace.

Then she said, "And you, sir, I am expecting you to be careful all the way to New Orleans and back. Now, get out of here, before I start to cry." That went without saying because she was already crying by the time Troy let her go.

The two spare two horses were already tied to the rear of the wagon, so Troy and Aubrey saddled up. Don got in the driver's seat of the wagon, and they rolled out toward Chihuahua. All four of them were crying a little as they left the camp.

The main trail was a quarter mile or so from the river, as they left town. The trail alternated between being soft sand and rough, hard ground. The sand was much better, except in those areas where it was so deep the trailer wheels bogged down.

An hour or so into the ride, Troy tied his horse to the wagon and got on the driver's seat with Don. He said, "How is everything going with the wagon?"

"I hate to brag, Troy, but Aubrey and I did a great piece of work on this wagon. I do not want to jinx it by saying too much. So far, the wagon is giving me a smooth ride. I have no complaints. And we are rolling at a good clip, so 'Chihuahua, here we come.'"

"That sounds great! I would love to get to Chihuahua as soon as possible. I told Bill that we would try to be there for a couple of weeks. Now, I am thinking that one week will be enough. However, there may be reasons to stay there longer. We will see. I know that Bill wants to show us some of the sights of his new home. We need to make sure to enjoy that as much as possible for Bill's sake. And I want us to spend some time with his family, to get to know them better. After a reasonable visit, I want to take off for the coast to catch a ship. Have you ever been on a ship?"

"No, neither Aubrey nor I have ever been on even a good-sized boat. And, frankly, I am a little worried about it. I hear that it takes a while to feel normal on a ship, and until then, you can be extremely sick. Is that correct?"

"Yes, unfortunately, that is correct. Usually, though, it is not that bad. And even if you get sick, you usually get over it in a half day or so. You really, never know. On my first ship, we were in rough water. I was sick for three days. Once I got well, I was never sick again, even in especially rough waters."

"I hope it is that way with me. I would not mind getting sick once if it was all over after that."

"I certainly hope any sea sickness is mild for all of us. It has been long enough since I sailed, that I am a little concerned I may get some sea sickness, at first. I hope not, but you just never know."

The first day went well. Most of the trail was smooth, there was no wind, to speak of. By nightfall, a full moon was up. The trail was visible, so they did not stop for supper. All of them ate some jerky and Justine's bread.

By about 10:00 o'clock, they stopped for the night. Camp was about a quarter mile from the river. Each man picked a soft spot under the wagon.

Next morning, Troy was up early again making coffee. As Don and Aubrey got up, Aubrey said, "Troy, I think we made a good many miles yesterday. Were you satisfied with how far we have gone?"

"Yes, I am satisfied with yesterday. I certainly hope we can make that many miles every day. I realize some days will not work that well. All we can do is work hard and push forward, but not wear out the horses.

"Oh, and we need to stay vigilant and watch for danger along the way. We know there might be thieves and Indians. Wild animals can also be a problem. And we need to remember what Bill said about the one rocky area with an overabundance of rattlesnakes. We especially need to be careful to watch for places that might cause a wagon break-down. None of us will ever forget your accident, Don, as we were headed to Santa Fe. We certainly do not want that to happen again."

Don was thrown off a wagon, he was driving, when there was sudden damage to the front-end. He was unconscious for days and it was miraculous he survived.

A cup of coffee and a chunk of bread was everybody's breakfast. Then they got hitched up and were on the road.

The weather over the past month had been warm and dry. Today promised to be wet. The clouds increased to the point that they all stopped and got their slickers out.

It was good the slickers were brought out because when the rain started, it came hard and fast. The brothers were able to get in amongst some trees as the rain was starting. The rain stopped after an hour and the guys got back underway.

As night came on, the overcast sky made them decide against traveling in the dark. They would start earlier in the morning if the moon was up.

They had a small campfire for coffee that evening.

As they sat around the fire, Troy said, "Guys, I may be wrong about this, but from the description Bill gave me of the place where they were attacked by Indians, I think we are camping on it. That probably should not concern us much because he thought it was an accident the Indians happened upon them here. They apparently were a hunting party and likely a long way from their homes."

With that uncomforting thought in their heads, they settled down for the night.

The clouds broke during the night and the moon was just as

bright as the night before, so Troy decided they should move on. He had the third watch that night, so was already up.

There was no campfire or coffee. The guys had the last of Justine's first loaf of bread as they hitched up the wagon and saddled the horses.

As Don walked around camp, he found a broken arrow with a metal point. "Hey, Troy, look at this arrow I found. It may be a coincidence, but it looks like the kind Bill described, doesn't it?"

"It sure does, Don. Hey, since we are ready to go, I think we should get started. I could not sleep very well last night, despite me saying it should be safe. It just felt creepy knowing what happened here."

"I agree," said Aubrey. "I think we should roll out of here."

The morning went well. There was no more rain. A stage-coach, coming from the other way, stopped them mid-morning to see how conditions ahead had been.

Troy told them that it had been quiet along the trail since they left Albuquerque. The stagecoach driver, Harry Harrison, told them the past two days had been good for them. The day prior to that, they had been harassed by a gang of ruffians. But their man riding shotgun, Cliff Gates, was well known in the area. His presence, once it was known, caused the gang to re-think their position and leave.

Camp that night was set a couple hundred yards from the river, in a grove of trees. The sky looked like it might rain again. It looked worse this night than the prior night, so rain might not be the worst of it. Camping in the trees was an attempt to have a little cover from the rain, particularly if it turned into a storm.

Watch was kept all night, as usual, mainly in case there was a storm coming through, but also to protect against possible attack from ruffians of any kind.

Don was the first to get up. He restarted the campfire they had built the night before and started a pot of coffee. Troy and

Aubrey got up quickly when they smelled the coffee. They walked slowly to the campfire.

"Good morning, guys," Don said. "Did you sleep well?"

"Yes, I did," said Aubrey. "I slept like a rock most of the night. Well, whenever I was not standing watch, that is. I am more than happy to stand guard duty, especially with what we heard about thieves being in the area."

The trail was smooth most of the day. The guys were making good time, from what they could determine, by looking for landmarks. A short lunch was consumed near what they thought was the snake-infested area mentioned by both Bill and Justine. Nobody tried to look for any snakes. It looked like the rocky kind of area where snakes would live.

After their lunch, the brothers hit the trail hard to make as much distance as possible. The wagon had slowed them down. That could not be helped. Still, they were moving as fast as they could without damaging the wagon.

Nightfall found them on a relatively smooth trail with enough light to continue their journey. They finally stopped about 9:00 pm, made camp, and had a little supper. It was funny, but the harder they rode, the less they wanted to eat. So, as they had been doing lately, a light supper was nibbled on and they got in their bedrolls.

Troy was standing watch about 1:00 am when a bright light caught his eye. On a tall hill across the river, there appeared what looked like an Indian chief dressed all in white sitting astride a white horse. He was carrying a long fighting lance with white material down the shaft. It was unbelievable.

After staring at it for ten minutes, he decided he should wake Don and Aubrey. Before he was able to wake them, the vision disappeared.

When Don took over the shift at 2:00 am, Troy explained what he had seen. Don had a hard time deciding to believe him, so Troy asked him to keep looking over the river to see if the vision came back. It never did.

Over breakfast the guys discussed the night and Troy's vision.

"Next time, you should wake us," said Aubrey. "I would fall down in shock if I saw something like that. Do you suppose it was some kind of sign? We are about to lose the river and go across a dry sandy desert for about three days. I certainly hope that is not a sign of bad luck along the way."

"I do not know about bad luck," said Don; "but it does sound like the Jornada Del Muerto will be the toughest part of our journey. We will ride through the desert without any place to fill our water barrels. Thank goodness for the wagon. We would really have trouble keeping track of enough water for three days, if we only had the horses."

"You are certainly right," said Troy. "I am glad we brought a large water barrel."

"Yeh, me too," said Aubrey.

They had a quick breakfast and were on their way. It was obvious when they started into the Jornada Del Muerto. The countryside almost at once turned very sandy. Most of the ground they had been riding over since they left Albuquerque was sandy, but not like this area. It was more like a large sand dune by a body of water.

There was still plant life but different. The wagon driver had to be especially careful to keep the wagon wheels from bogging down in the deep sand. The trail tried to keep away from deep sand, but there were areas where it was unavoidable.

The first night camp was made by a group of salt cedars in a low area off to the side of the trail. As usual the guys drove themselves until late at night. They finally stopped for fear they would get into deep sand without realizing it.

Around a small campfire, Troy said, "Well, this has been an interesting day. I have not seen that much sand since my sailing days. Back then, as we were sailing along the coast, there were places where huge sand dunes made a barrier along the coast. There are more plants in this sand. I suppose the coastal dunes must come and go according to the storms coming in from the sea."

"Did you ever get caught in a bad storm while you were out at sea?" asked Aubrey.

"I did once. Our ship was sailing south down the east coast of Florida when we sailed into a storm coming from the southeast. We tried to sail out to sea, hoping to get around it. It was so large that it finally became clear that sailing around it would be impossible, unless we sailed half the way to Spain and then turn south. And it also was going to be impossible to turn north and get back to a safe port because the storm was moving too fast.

"Finally, the captain turned back to the south into the storm and tried to steer toward the weakest part. That did not work like he wanted, but we eventually got through it. We found safer water along the coast after the storm had had its way with us and went on by."

Don asked, "What was going through a bad storm like?"

"It was awful. Even men who had been sailing the longest were having trouble keeping the least bit of food down. The ones of us who had been sailing a year threw up until there was nothing left to throw up. You need to be strong or you will get to the point where you are sick for so long that you would not mind just dying. Juan Leos and I went through that storm together and it was the end of our sailing careers. After we got back to shore, neither of us wanted to sail any more. That is when Juan went back to Santa Fe, and I settled in New Orleans."

"Have either of you been on a ship since that storm?" Aubrey asked.

"I do not think so. I know I have not and as far as I know Juan has not either."

Don said, "Troy, you have been talking about leaving Chihuahua and going back to New Orleans by ship. Are you not concerned about that? I originally was not, but now that you have told me your story, I am beginning to get a little sick just thinking about it."

Troy laughed and said, "I guess that was a bad idea telling you guys that story. I am not really concerned about sailing across the gulf. It does not usually get the ferocious weather that the east coast gets. Oh, it can have bad weather but not as bad as the Atlantic. I think we will be alright. One reason why I wanted to sail back across the gulf was that I always heard how calm it was. It does not have the huge swells that the Atlantic does because it is not as deep as the Atlantic.

"I do predict that you will both be sick for the first few days, but hopefully everything after that will be alright. Most people are only sick for a short time and then their bodies adjust to the rolling and tossing of the ships."

The second day in the Jornada del Muerto was much like the first, except for two places with especially deep sand. The wagon almost got stuck at one point. Troy, who was driving, managed to get through it. Once he realized what was happening, he steered the wagon over some small shrubs. There was more firm ground there that helped him get past the sand without any further problem.

In the afternoon, they met a family group of ten headed north. They were going to a wedding in Socorro. The group were from Las Cruces and said they had not had any trouble along the way. The Rampys were the first people they had seen.

The brothers continued late into the evening and finally stopped when the moon went down. The darkness prevented them from seeing the trail. It was especially dark that evening. The stars were amazing.

Their Dad had taught them about many constellations, so they sat up late talking about the ones they were seeing. When they finally got into their bedrolls, Don stayed up for the first watch.

Since he had already been staring at the sky, he saw meteor after meteor fall in a shower like he had never seen before. He would have woken up Troy and Aubrey, if they had not already stayed up much longer than normal.

"You guys should have seen the meteor shower last night," Don said while they were having their morning coffee. "I have never seen anything like it. I can remember seeing a few meteors fall on dark nights back home. Then it was usually only one meteor or two and that was it. Las night, I saw dozens.

"I am glad that I did not see a vision last night, Troy, like you did four or five days ago. It was already sort of mystical with the meteor shower. A vision of any kind would have made me wake you guys up, just for comfort."

They all laughed, and Troy said, "When I saw that vision, it was not creepy at all. Really, it was sort of awe inspiring and soothing at the same time. A message of comfort was what it seemed to be. I did not realize that at first, but once I thought about it for a while, that is what it seemed to be. So, if you see one some time, I bet it would not bother you at all."

By evening they had gotten out of the desert and passed the turnoff to Las Cruces. They camped in a grove of trees near the river. The next day, they were hoping to reach El Paso. From there it would not be far to Chihuahua.

As they ate the last of Justine's bread for breakfast, Troy said, "Well, guys I think this part of the trip is rapidly coming to an end. Hopefully, this afternoon we will get to El Paso. I understand that we will cross the river there. Apparently, it changes course and heads more southeast. Our course will continue directly to the south. Depending on how much we push it, we might be in Chihuahua in a few more days. I would like to stay with Bill and Frances a week or ten days at the most. Then we will leave and head to Matamoros. I know I should get you guys on a ship as quickly as I can, so you do not back out on me. Especially now that I have told you my bad weather story."

Aubrey said, "Oh, I do not think we will back out on you. Troy. Sailing does seem to have its problems, but is much quicker than horseback."

"Yes, that is the way I see it too, Troy," said Don.

By late afternoon, they got to the river crossing. The water was a little higher at the crossing than they were expecting, but they did not hesitate and went on across.

It was getting close to the end of the day, and they could have made camp for the night and crossed the river in the morning when the horses were fresher. Experience had taught them that crossing a stream when the horses were already warm was much better than getting them to cross before they warmed up.

Like most days on this journey, the brothers continued until the evening was getting too dark to see the trail.

In the Chihuahuan desert, it was difficult to find a grove of trees to camp in. The best they could do was a group of large cactus-like plants. Vegetation there was much different than anything they had seen before. It was certainly different. Not knowing the names of any of the plants was frustrating. They began to wonder what kind of world Bill was living in. Hopefully, he could give them an orientation about the plants and animals of the fascinating countryside.

The next morning, after at least two cups of coffee and the horses were saddled, Troy got in the driver's seat of the wagon, and they were on their way. Chihuahua was drawing them onward. Troy was wanting to only spend a short time there, but something about this new adventure was too compelling to let them stay only a few days.

By nightfall they could tell the destination was near. They decided to make camp and get some rest. Pushing hard the past two weeks had worn all of them to a frazzle. A good night's sleep was something they all needed. The next night they, hopefully, would be sleeping in their brother Bill's new hometown.

8 | CHIHUAHUA

They were up with the sun even though they spent more time than normal sitting around the campfire talking. The trip from New Orleans to Santa Fe was their main topic of conversation. It had been an unbelievable trip in many ways. That is the trip that almost killed Don when he fell headfirst from the seat of a wagon he was driving. Everyone was thankful that he was finally alright after about four weeks. Most of that time, he was completely unconscious, and it appeared he would probably die.

Finally, the conversation turned to their rushed trip to Chihuahua. The trip had been a blur and it was about over. A few more hours today and they should be there, rejoicing in their brother Bill's new hometown.

After finally getting off to a rather slow start, they enjoyed the final five miles or so into Chihuahua. It was a pleasant ride. The brothers had been enjoying the desert scenery in recent days. The variety of plants was like nothing they had ever seen before. There were both tall and short plants. Some of the plants were succulents and cactus. The others were not easy to describe and looked somewhat like palm trees, except shorter.

The road had been busy as they got closer to town. Ten houses were scattered up close to the road once they had gotten within a mile or so from town. Every house had a yard with kids playing and dogs barking. All the children were friendly and waved excitedly.

There were nine different people on the road. They appeared to be mainly farmers taking fruits or vegetables to town for sale.

Finally, the three brothers, who were getting more excited by the minute, topped one last hill, and there was Chihuahua in front of them. They had known they were getting close because from several miles away the steeple from the cathedral was visible at times.

They hurried down into town, with a renewed excitement. It was lunch time. Their intention was to find Bill before they decided to eat something. The main road went right by the cathedral. Past that were many businesses that looked especially busy at this time of day.

Troy thought he would recognize Claudio's store when they got to it. Claudio was a dry goods dealer, just like Troy. The two of them had discussed the business a great deal while they were together in Santa Fe. They had become friends.

As he was remembering a few of the differences in their businesses, he realized they were approaching it. The store was about three hundred feet ahead of them, on the right. It also appeared that Bill and Claudio were standing by the front door discussing something. They did not see Bill's brothers as they rode up in front of the store because they were both talking to a customer.

Troy yelled to them, "Hey, have you gentlemen got any fruit tree seedlings? I have been thinking about planting a small orchard."

Bill turned quickly. Spotting his brothers, he laughed and said, "We do not have any seedlings at this very moment, but we should be getting some soon. How many would you like?"

Troy said, "I'll take about five hundred, if you will plant them for me."

Then they all laughed. The guys dismounted and grabbed Bill and Claudio for a round of big hugs.

Bill said, "It is great to see you guys. I was beginning to think you had gone back to New Orleans the way we had come, through St. Louis."

"Oh, we would have been here sooner," Don said, "but we had to allow time for Troy to fall in love and for his sweetheart time to kill someone."

Both Bill and Claudio stood there looking shocked, wondering what they were talking about.

Bill said, "Maybe you guys should explain a bit about that last thing you mentioned. Now, I knew that Troy seemed a little sweet on Justine Martinez before we left Albuquerque. What else happened? On second thought, maybe we had better wait until Frances gets here with lunch and then you can tell her also. After all, Justine is Frances's cousin."

"Then again," Bill added, "If Justine killed someone, maybe you should tell us all a little of the story before you spring it on us all at once."

Don said, "A bad guy who used to live in town, but had been gone for a while, came back. Late one afternoon, when Justine's store was empty, he came in, forced her into the back room and attacked her. Troy came in about that time and they got in a vicious fight. Justine thought the other guy was going to kill Troy with a knife, so she picked up a pistol off the floor and shot the man."

"Goodness, that is hard to believe," said Bill. "I would not have thought that Justine could shoot someone, even in self-defense."

Troy said, "She is a lot stronger than she seems. And she can do anything she puts her mind to."

"So, Troy," asked Claudio, "Is it true that you and Justine are in love?"

Troy blushed and chuckled and finally said, "Oh, I am pretty sure I love her, but I am not entirely certain that she loves me."

Aubrey said, "Don and I saw them kissing one day and it looked like love to us. And I am thinking that if we can get him to New Orleans and back to Albuquerque, there definitely will be another wedding to go to in our future."

They all laughed, and Troy blushed even brighter than before.

Troy spoke up and said, "I think we had better go find us some lunch, so that we can change the subject."

Bill saw Frances driving her buggy up the street and said, "Here comes lunch now, so we can stay on this subject for a while longer." That drew another laugh from everyone.

Frances was excited to see her new brothers-in-law. She hugged everyone while Bill took a big pot of chili into the back room of the store for lunch.

She said, "How were your last weeks in Albuquerque? What did you do?"

Don as usual had to toss another barb at Troy. He said, "Well, while Aubrey and I worked, Troy fell in love. And he tried to get himself killed too."

"Maybe one of you needs to tell me more. I seem to have missed a lot by coming home."

Bill stepped in about that time to clarify the story as well as he knew it.

"Wow," said Frances as she wiped tears from her eyes. "Knowing how sweet and gentle Justine is, she must have felt horrible after that."

Troy finally spoke, "She certainly did. For most of the time we were still there, she had a hard time living with the fact that she had killed someone. Of course, she was glad that she saved my life, but the idea of killing someone was something that she had never even thought about. I do think she was feeling better by the time we left. I was thinking we should stay there another week or two, but she ran us off."

"Why did she do that?" Bill asked.

"It was really kind of sweet," Troy said. "Justine said the sooner we left, the quicker we would be back. So, it is nice to know she wants us back."

Aubrey and Don laughed. Then Aubrey said, "I am not sure if she cares whether Don and I come back or not. It is obviously Troy that she wants back. The two of them seemed to have developed a certain bond with each other."

Troy turned red again. He finally said with a chuckle, "Can you blame her for thinking that I am handsome and charming?"

Everyone laughed then.

"OK, I think I get the picture," Bill said. "So, how would you all like some chili? It is probably different than you have ever eaten before. I think it is great. Frances and her mother both make a chili with lots of locally ground peppers and meat, usually lamb. Oh, one warning, it may be a little hotter than you are used to."

"Don't worry about that," said Aubrey. "We ate gallons of chili in Albuquerque. It was hot as blazes at first, but we got used to it before we left for Chihuahua."

The group ate the entire pot of chili with no complaints. Then Bill and Frances showed them around town. They showed them the center of town where many of the shops were. Then they went by the school at the cathedral where Frances was teaching. After that Frances showed them a few of her favorite parts of town. They ended at their home in town where Bill and Frances were staying most of the time. Frances's parents were living at the ranch.

Troy and his brothers spent the night at Bill and Frances's home in town.

The next day Troy enjoyed the day with Claudio in the store discussing their two businesses. The businesses were different in many ways, yet amazingly similar in other ways.

Claudio served his community with anything that was needed and could be brought into town by traders. He sold groceries, clothes, hardware, and even small farming equipment.

In New Orleans, Troy sold many of the same things, plus trapping and traveling equipment. Both men were good at business and knew their respective markets.

Claudio came here from Spain with his family. Their business at first was growing fruit orchards. His family had done that for centuries in Spain and parts of France.

After Claudio started growing fruit orchards, they built a farm headquarters about two miles outside town. Then later they opened a small store in town. And even later than that, they built a home in town and started living there most of the time to stay near the store.

Troy had left home when he was young and went to the east coast of the United States to find work. He sailed on merchant ships for a year or so. Those ships transported goods from Boston, down around the tip of Florida and up to New Orleans, and beyond.

The ships would carry all kinds of goods, everything from grains and livestock to furniture and machinery. Troy eventually learned a great deal about the business of transporting and selling a wide variety of merchandise. Finally, he decided he would rather sell the goods than transport them.

After an unusually rough storm that almost took their lives, Troy and his friend, Juan Leos, who he had met on the ship, decided they had sailed long enough.

Troy got off the ship for the final time at the port of New Orleans, with plans to open a dry goods store. He still owns the store. It is being run by two partners that (he is hoping) will want to buy him out when he returns.

Juan sailed farther along the coast before he finally quit. He stopped at Matamoros, a location that was as close as he could get to Santa Fe. There he got off the ship and made his way home.

Once home, Juan started doing what Troy intended to do. He started a trading post north of Santa Fe, between there and Taos.

Juan was at the trading post, several years later, when Bill Rampy came looking for "his brother Troy's friend." They became great friends and worked together that winter. In January, they went with other Santa Fe merchants to a trade fair in Chihuahua.

That trade fair is where Bill met Juan's cousin, Frances, and they fell in love.

Don and Aubrey spent more time with Bill seeing Chihuahua and the surrounding countryside. They returned to Claudio's store at the end of the day. Then everyone rode out to Claudio and Anita's rancho for the evening.

Aubrey was riding next to Troy and Claudio. He asked, "How have you gentlemen been today? Troy, I assume you have learned a lot about doing business in Chihuahua."

"It has been an exceptionally good day. I have learned a lot. Claudio obviously sells many of the same things that I do, but from different suppliers and manufacturers. It seems like a completely different store at first, but once you look at it a little closer, the similarities are amazing. I guess, it points out that people have many of the same needs, no matter where they are."

"Hey, look at that smoke up ahead," Bill yelled. "It looks like it is near the barn. We had better get there quickly to see what is burning."

They were only a half mile from the rancho and got there quickly. There was smoke pouring out of the back of the horse barn.

Claudio got to the corral first. He ran into the barn first to check on the horses. There were six horses in stalls that he released. They quickly galloped out into the corral.

Bill, Aubrey, and Don rode around the barn to where the

smoke was coming from. A lean-to shed attached to the back of the barn had smoke billowing out. The shed had tools and a small amount of hay inside. The hay had caught fire.

Bill and Don used two shovels lying near the garden to throw dirt on the fire. It was out in minutes. It could have consumed the entire barn if they had not seen the smoke when they did.

"I wonder how that started," asked Don. "I don't see anything around here that might have started a fire."

Bill said, "I saw some lightning over this way a few hours ago. It must have been a small thunderstorm. We never got a storm in town. I bet that lightning hit the shed and lit a tiny ember that slowly grew into the fire we saw."

"I think you are right, Bill," said Claudio as he walked around the shed. "Look at this scorch mark on the side of the shed. We need to check this again, after supper, to make sure there is no more smoke or heat coming out of the shed."

Bill said, "Sounds good to me. Hey, while we are out here, why don't we show everybody your horses?"

"Those are beautiful horses," said Troy. "I saw them as Claudio released them from their stalls."

As the group walked around to the corral, Claudio explained that the horses were Andalusians.

Claudio said, "My brother raises these horses in Spain and has sent us several over the years. We have carried on the breeding here, but have only sold a few. We like these horses so much that we would rather keep them than sell them. You will all have to ride one before you leave for America. They are special."

"We would love to ride one," Aubrey said.

"Yes, we certainly would," added Don.

After having supper on the back porch of the house, Bill, and Frances, showed Troy, Aubrey, and Don around the ranch headquarters. "Well, I guess I can skip showing you the barn while we look around, since you have already been there. It mainly is filled with horse stalls, hay, and riding equipment. If we had not gotten that fire out soon enough, we would have all seen the biggest fire of our lives. With as much hay as there is in that barn, it would have been burning for days.

"Over past the barn is the smallest of four orchards. I think you have heard the story of why Claudio and Anita came here from Spain in the first place. They came to grow fruit, which they have done now for twenty-five years. And they still grow some fruit, but not to the extent they originally did. They grow now just for local people, friends, and family. There are two orchards here at the headquarters and two more a mile to the west, in a beautiful valley.

"I told you earlier that Frances and I are living in her parents' house in town now. Soon we intend to start building a house here at the rancho. You can see that area to the east of the house where we have put in stakes to mark the site. We wanted it to be close to the main house, so Frances can help her mother. It would be especially helpful for family gatherings. And Anita will be able to help us with children if we are blessed with them." Bill chuckled and said, "I think Anita would really like lots of grandchildren."

That got a laugh from everybody.

Troy finally said, "What mother would not want grandchildren? And we brothers would not mind some nieces or nephews to play with some day. Bill, you do know how that all works, don't you?"

Everyone laughed. Even Bill laughed. And Frances blushed.

"Yes, we do know how it works to have kids. And we are doing our best. In fact, we are hopeful that Frances is with child now.

"And if she is, you guys had better hurry to New Orleans, or our baby might be here before you get back."

Everyone congratulated the two of them and clapped Bill on the back.

Troy added, "Hopefully our trip to New Orleans will be over

quicker than you think. If we can make connections easily and quickly at Matamoros with a merchant ship, the trip should not take long."

Bill asked, "What made you decide to sail part way back to New Orleans?"

"Oh, when I was sailing, I enjoyed it, most of the time. I just thought I would like to do it again. And I thought it would be fun to introduce Aubrey and Don to sailing. Also, I always wanted to sail across the Gulf of Mexico. And that is what we would be doing to get back to New Orleans. Of course, the ship would probably sail along the coast without taking a direct route to the city. But that would still be fun. I could tell myself that we sailed across the gulf, even with a slightly less than direct route."

"Wow, that sounds exciting guys," Bill said. "I hope you do have fun… and a safe trip. But, if you want to beat little Rampy, you had better hurry every chance you get."

Aubrey said, "Bill, I am sure we will. If there is going to be a new Rampy in Chihuahua, that is something we will all want to see!"

"When are you guys leaving? I know there are several of our local attractions you will want to see before you can leave. Let's discuss that in the morning and we will work out a plan to give you a tour as quickly as possible. Of course, we certainly do not want to rush you off. We want you to stay if you would like. If you want to beat the baby, you probably should not stay here too long."

Troy said, "I agree completely that we had better get to moving as quickly as we can. There are several more things around town that I think we would like to see. We can discuss that in the morning, get them seen, and be on our way to New Orleans."

Bill said, "We probably should get started for town before it gets too dark."

The next morning, Frances and Bill were up early getting breakfast and coffee ready. It was not long until the smells of breakfast got Troy up, and then Don and Aubrey.

"That coffee smells great, Frances," said Troy. "Did you make it or did Bill?"

"Do you think there would be a difference if I made it Troy?" asked Bill.

"Oh, no I guess not. I was just thinking that with as many days as you have spent on the trail, you might make 'trail coffee', and as sophisticated as Frances is, she would probably make 'city coffee'. Either way, I am excited to have a cup."

"Ok, well here you go Troy," Bill said, handing him a cup.

Troy stared at the cup a long minute, blew on it for a minute and then took a sip. He said, "There is no doubt that this is the finest coffee I have ever drank. Thank you both."

Bill said, "Troy, what do you think you would like to see around here before you head for Matamoros? I think you have seen most of the town."

"I think we can plan to see the beautiful valley that someone mentioned, when we come back through. The only thing I would like to see before we leave is the cavern you mentioned. That sounds especially interesting. But after we see that, maybe we had better leave for the coast. There is no telling how long we will need to wait there before an eastbound ship comes by.

"Bill, I would like to spend some more time with you and Claudio in the store. And I think Don and Aubrey also had that in mind. Do you think that you and Frances could show us the cavern tomorrow? Then we would leave the next day."

"I am sure we can work that out tomorrow, Troy."

Don and Aubrey had come in and started working on their own cups of coffee as Bill and Troy were finishing their planning. They were all in agreement to leave for the coast the day after tomorrow if they could see the cavern tomorrow.

The day was spent by all the guys in and around the area of Claudio's store.

Troy was especially interested in who Claudio's suppliers

were and where they were located. He knew that he might be working with many of the same businesses once he got established in Albuquerque. Even though the war for independence was over and Mexico was now an independent country, that should not affect many of the independent suppliers. Of course, there would be new suppliers soon coming into Mexico from all over the United States. The merchants would deal with those changes as they came about.

Don and Aubrey were most interested in Claudio's inventory and how he handled it. Unlike Troy, they were not as interested in where it all came from, but rather how it was managed once it got to Claudio's store. Especially intriguing was how Claudio handled weapons and related equipment. A few weapons were kept on the main floor for display. The balance was kept in a basement below the backroom to keep them safe from anyone who might want to steal them.

The day was long, but fulfilling to all the men. Troy, particularly, felt he had learned a great deal about how Claudio ran his businesses and some things he might need to know in Albuquerque.

Supper was eaten at Bill and Frances's house. Anita and Claudio both came for supper also. They talked for a long time, mostly about Troy, Aubrey, and Don's coming trip to New Orleans and their return.

The trip to New Orleans was obviously going to be largely a sea voyage, but the return trip was undetermined. If they came back by sea, the trip would bring them back by Chihuahua. A cross country trip would not.

Troy said, "Going across the Gulf of Mexico is exciting to me. Of course, I know there are risks involved, but there are likely more risks coming cross country. In taking goods cross country by wagon, you can have a broken wagon or injured driver. You can also have all kinds of threats along the way, such as, Indians, outlaws, range fires, buffalo stampedes, thunder and lightning. In the ocean, generally the only problems are bad storms. There used to be serious problems with pirates or privateers. But apparently that is not the problem it once was."

"Speaking of that," Claudio interrupted, "there have been a few people in the store this past month that mentioned a group of banditos operating in the area this side of Matamoros. Apparently, several individuals or small groups have been attacked. I think one man was killed and two more injured."

"Thanks for letting us know about that, Claudio," said Troy. "That is directly in our path. We will need to be especially careful in that area. The horses we will be riding are some of the best available, providing we don't get boxed in. We should be able to outrun most groups."

Claudio added, "There are a couple of short stretches of canyons along the route to Matamoros, so those are areas to look out for. Most of the trip will be wide open."

"That is good to know," said Aubrey. "The last thing we need is a bullet wound."

After that thought settled in a bit, Claudio said, "I understand you will be going to the cavern tomorrow. I hope you enjoy it. That cavern is truly one of the treasures around here. It is beautiful, mystical, and amazing, all at the same time. It was thrilling the first time I saw it. I could not believe a place like that existed, but it obviously does. The cavern is a good thing to see at the end of your trip to Chihuahua. It should make you want to come back soon, just to see it again. But we are certainly glad that you have other reasons to come here. We will be glad to see you when you get back from New Orleans."

The next morning, after a large breakfast made by Frances, Bill led his three brothers east out of Chihuahua to the cavern. It only took about thirty minutes to get to the cavern. They stopped near an opening at the base of a high hill.

"Guys, this is Nombre de Dios (Name of God) caves. It is amazing inside. I could barely believe it the first time Frances and I came here. Unfortunately, we cannot go in this entrance because it takes special equipment to go in this way. It is sort of like mountain climbing, except on the inside of the mountain. We will need to go up this hill and go into another entrance. At that point we will see a lot of amazing things, just not as amazing as we would see by going into this entrance. So, follow me and we will go up to the other entrance. It is about a half mile more. At that point, we will need to light our torches and then go into a cave. It is extremely dark without a torch."

At the cavern entrance, they lit the torches by a spark from a flint. The torches were liberally coated with an oily substance.

"OK, everybody, please follow me," Bill said. "You will be able to feel a temperature change a little way into the cavern. The temperature in the cavern stays steady all the time. So, if it is hot outside, you will feel the temperature go down. If it is cold outside, you will feel the temperature in the cavern get warmer."

Everybody mentioned when they could feel the change of temperature. As they walked on, beautiful cave formations began to be seen. Most of them were wet. Bill told them what he remembered about limestone deposits in the cave water forming the interesting shapes and colors. Many of the formations came in a variety of colors. Most of them were the color of plain limestone, tan, but others were anything from red to brown.

When they finally had gone as far into the cave as it was possible to go, they stopped. Bill said, "This is the end of the upper trail. Please sit down for a few minutes. You can see why we think the cavern is special. It is an amazing collection of shapes and colors. Apparently, the lower cavern is much more spectacular than this one. We will sit here for a few minutes to enjoy the sights and listen to how quiet it is here. Then we will leave before our torches start to go out. If we had no light in here, it would be almost impossible to get out. The cavern is as dark as a place can be. You would have to feel your way out if there was no light."

Over supper at the rancho later, Frances said, "Bill tells me that you all enjoyed the caverns. What did you like the most?"

Troy said, "I enjoyed it all. I did not know that anything like that really exists. It was almost magical. Bill explained to us, sort of how the formations came to be, but I still could barely believe they were real."

"I agree," said Don. "I could barely believe they were real. But you had to believe because they were right there in front of you. All I have to say is, wow, that was amazing."

Aubrey said, "I agree. It was unbelievably amazing."

Anita, Claudio, and Frances were all laughing at the comments. They had been to the cavern many times and knew how fantastic they were.

Claudio said, "I have never told my family this, but when I was a young man, I tried to go into the lower cavern and came close to killing myself."

Anita sat there with a shocked look on her face. She apparently did not know either.

"I had a strong rope, but I did not use a good knot. The rope came loose when I was trying to climb down a cliff. I fell, of course; but I am not sure how far. It was maybe twenty feet, not nearly to the bottom of the cliff. I fell onto a small ledge. It was so dark in the cavern I was not aware the little ledge was there.

"It scared me so bad, that all I could do was lay there and shake. If not for that little ledge, I knew I would have been dead, and my family would never have known what happened to me. That thought terrified me.

"After I quit shaking, I got to my feet and was able to find a way to climb back to where I started from. I went home, put my rope in the barn and never went into that part of the cave again."

Frances and Anita were both crying by the time Claudio's story was finished. They both got up from their chairs slowly and gave Claudio a hug and told him they were glad he made it out safe. Anita also slapped him on the arm as she walked away.

Claudio's confession brought the evening to a close. It was late, so Anita and Claudio spent the night at the house also.

9 | HEADING TO THE SEA

Frances and her mother fixed a large breakfast for Bill's brothers as they got ready to leave Chihuahua and go to New Orleans. Their first goal was getting to Matamoros and attempting to find a cargo ship heading east.

The brothers had their gear packed and their horses ready to go by the time breakfast was on the table. They were not taking much gear, only camping equipment and food. Each brother was going to be trailing a horse behind the horse he was riding. All six horses were sturdy and fast. The spare horses were carrying the gear and food, but were not outfitted as packhorses.

After breakfast and several cups of coffee, all seven of them went out onto the back porch. The horses were waiting a few yards away.

Bill spoke first. He said, "I cannot tell you how much I appreciate you coming to see us. And I sincerely hope you will come back as soon as you can. I understand you might decide to take a different route back to Albuquerque, so we might not see you again this trip.

"It has been a pleasure to have you here. I hope and pray

that you make it to New Orleans and then back to Albuquerque safely. And please let us know, if you and Justine do decide to get married. We would love to come to the wedding."

Troy said, "Bill, Frances, Anita, and Claudio, we loved being here and wish we could stay longer. However, we need to get our journey and some business completed. If we do not come by here on the return trip, we will certainly come back as soon as we can. And yes, if I can talk Justine into marrying me, we will let you know. I guess we had better get on the trail to Matamoros. God bless you all. Be safe. And we will be back as soon as we can."

After that, there was a jumble of conversation and hugging. The brothers got on their horses and headed out of town.

There was no wagon this time. Each brother rode their favorite horse with another sturdy, fast horse trailing behind. All three of them carried their favorite pistols and each of the six horses carried two rifles and extra ammunition.

Once outside town, they rode at a pace they felt the horses could maintain all day. They followed the established trail to the southeast. They would follow that trail until they got to the area of the mission at Torreon. Then they would turn east toward Matamoros.

The trail they intended to follow was not the most direct way to Matamoros, but it had the advantage of avoiding some of the worst desert in the area. It was also the most popular route and the smoothest. They rode close enough to each other so that they could talk without yelling.

Troy said, "I asked Claudio, a few days ago, if we would be likely to run into problems along the route to Matamoros. He said there had been reports of banditos between Torreon and Matamoros. The reports said the banditos usually attacked slow moving groups that had wagons. So, I think we need to be on the lookout for trouble; but not overly worried about being attacked. Claudio also said it was important to avoid ambush spots. He said to be especially careful at pinch points between rocky areas and along narrow valleys. I would like to see us get safely on a ship at Matamoros and make it to New Orleans as quickly as possible. We need to keep focused on any area that could be a problem."

Aubrey said, "Troy, you have plenty of experience on ships. And the idea of sailing across the Gulf of Mexico does not worry you a bit. But the idea of that scares me to death. When we were riding those steamboats up and down the Mississippi and Missouri rivers, I had difficulty keeping my wits about me. But, acting like a sissy did not seem to be an option, when I was around so many other men. And at least the steamboats were not so far from shore. I always assumed I could swim to shore if I had to. But I am thinking that a ship sailing across the gulf would not even be in sight of the shore part of the time. So, with all that said, would you tell us what it is like to sail in a ship on the open ocean."

"Sure Aubrey. I am sorry. I did not think that you and Don might be concerned about the crossing. When I first got on a ship, I was more concerned about getting sick than I was about my safety. The ships seemed rather large to me, so I never even thought about them being unsafe in some way. Sea sickness did bother me for about three days, as I recall. When I felt better again, I never did think about other concerns on the ship."

Don asked, "How long will the ships be, Troy? And what was the worst storm you ever went through?"

Troy said, "The ships are usually eighty to one hundred feet; but they can be bigger and smaller. Oh, there was one terrible storm that we got into off the coast of Florida, that did make me fear for the ship's safety and my life. The ship got caught in the middle of the storm and we had to fight it for several days. Finally, we got out of the storm when it settled down some. After that we got back to land as quickly as we could."

Aubrey asked, "Did the storm blow you way past where you intended to stop?"

"Yes," Troy continued, "The storm blew us past a couple of ports we intended to stop at to drop off cargo. The ship's captain decided to go back and pick up the ports we missed. Then we finished our route north. I stayed on the ship until it got back to New Orleans. I got off the ship there and decided to make the town my home. Juan got on another ship and sailed to Matamoros. From there, he headed home to Santa Fe. Juan and I had both thought about getting back to land and finding work, so that storm made us decide it was time. That storm was really something. They called it a hurricane. I had heard of them before, but that was the first one either Juan or I had seen. It made even the most experienced sailors seasick."

Aubrey said, "That really sounds terrible. What are the odds of us seeing a storm like that?"

Troy said, "I probably should not have told you about that storm. They really are rare. I am pretty sure that you will never see one. That story was meant to explain how safe ships are. Certainly, if they can sail through a terrible storm like that one and survive, they will survive almost anything."

Aubrey said, "I can believe that ships are safe, but the sea-sickness still concerns me. What do you think, Don?"

"Oh, I am concerned about that too. I figure all we can do is get on the ship and see what happens. I have heard that if you get sick, it should be over in a day or so. That does not sound too bad."

Aubrey asked, "Troy, do you think most ships will be sailing close to the coast or will they be sailing farther away out to sea?"

"Aubrey, it just depends on whether they are stopping at small ports along the way. We might catch a ship that is just going back and forth from Matamoros to New Orleans. If we catch a ship that is going directly, it might only take two weeks to get to New Orleans, but the ship would be farther out to sea. The other kind of route might take us three or four weeks. It would travel mainly along the coast.

"Speaking of ships, I am certainly looking forward to getting to the coast, so we can look for a ship. There is no telling how long we might have to wait. But we need to get there first. It sounds like the trip to Matamoros will take us about two weeks. Then we will see what happens."

Don said, "Troy, I have another question for you. Do you expect we will have to do any work on whatever ship we sail on? Aubrey and I certainly do not know how to do anything on a ship."

Troy laughed and said, "No, we should not have to do anything onboard a ship. The only reason we might have to would be if something happened to some of the crew and there were not enough to keep the ship sailing. That is unlikely."

"If we did need to do anything, the ship's captain or his first mate would give us directions as to how and when we should do it. Like I said, that is unlikely. But the positive side is that you could learn a new skill."

"Yeah right," said Don. "I wouldn't mind learning a new skill; but I just do not want to wreck a ship, especially with me as a passenger." They all laughed.

"Well, Don," Troy said, "Think of it this way, if you hire on as part of the crew, they would pay you. Otherwise, you pay them."

Don laughed and said, "Why would they hire someone with no experience?"

Troy said, "That is exactly how green Juan and I were when we got hired on to our first ship. If they need help, they will hire anybody that seems halfway normal. And sometimes they do not have to be normal. They just need to be breathing. Hopefully, the ship that we catch will have a full crew with experienced men."

"I would go for that," said Aubrey.

"Me too," said Don.

"There is no need to worry," said Troy. "It should all work

out fine. We will be in New Orleans before you guys know it."

The well-traveled trail allowed the brothers to ride as fast as they wanted to, and their horses would let them. It was a desert but not completely dry. Here and there was a spring supporting reeds, grasses, and other plants. There were even trees at some springs.

There were a variety of small animals and birds. Coyotes and foxes were common. Bobcats were not. There were ground squirrels, prairie dogs, mice, and other furry animals.

Roadrunners were common as well as robins, quail, meadowlarks, and other small birds. Pheasants and larger birds were never seen.

Fifty miles was a good guess for the mileage on the first day. Sixty miles was more likely on the second day.

Two groups of people, heading north, were seen on the first two days. They passed one group heading south on the second day. The group was slowed down by the two wagons they were driving.

The brothers usually talked to each group for a while, when they passed one going either way.

Troy talked to the slower group heading south. He mentioned what they had heard about banditos. They had heard the warning before, so they had more fire power than they would have under normal conditions.

Camp the first two nights was close to small springs, while camp the third night was a dry camp in a sandy area away from the trail. Just as they were starting to lay out their camp, Don killed two sidewinder rattlesnakes in the area, so they moved camp about a quarter mile. It seemed like a less snake friendly area.

The next morning, they skipped their normal coffee and ate jerky on the road. It was their intention to make another good distance, since the weather was especially nice. Sixty miles was what they were shooting for again. That was only an estimate based on the map they had been given by Bill. He had copied it from one that Claudio had gotten from a friend three years before.

Aubrey said, "Troy, are you thinking we will go back to Albuquerque by this same route? Or are you thinking we will go overland? Of course, I realize that we will need to bring a caravan, if you want to bring a lot of items for your new store."

"I suppose a caravan will be a necessity. I will need to get the store stocked as soon as I can. That would take twenty or more wagons full of goods and equipment. I am not sure I want to start out with a caravan that large. I was thinking we might go back with six wagons with a wide assortment of items. Then we could buy the rest of the things we need from other sources. Obviously, we know there will be other traders coming by from time to time.

"We could probably get six wagons on a ship and sail back to Matamoros; but we also could do it overland and that might make more sense. That can be figured out once the ship gets to New Orleans."

Don said, "Hey guys, look up ahead there. I see what may be an area that would provide a good spot for bushwhackers. I think it needs to be looked at closely when we get near it."

"I agree, Don," said Troy. "I am glad you saw that as we were going over this hill. It looks like there are a couple of wagons that will get there before we do. We will have to make sure they get through the area safely before we go through."

The trail continued through a series of low hills until the brothers had almost caught up with the wagons. The wagons were still about a half mile ahead when they entered what looked like a risky area. Almost immediately, fire erupted.

Troy said, "Come on, guys, they need help. Let's see what we can do."

The three of them raced ahead to help their fellow travelers.

As the trail circled around a hill, they could see the two wagons stopped on the trail with all the riders off the wagon for protection. They were shooting about halfway up a hill in front of them at several riflemen.

Aubrey shouted to his brothers, "We can go back. I saw a trail up to the top of the hill."

Troy and Don followed Aubrey's lead and they were able to get above the ambushers without being seen. The brothers got their rifles out and were able to stop two of the ambushers with single shots. The third ambusher was trying to leave his perch, when a deadly shot from the wagons knocked him off his horse.

Troy and his brothers mounted their horses and started back down the hill. They came around behind the wagons. The brothers were cautious, at first, but were waved on by wagon drivers.

The brothers talked to the people in the caravan, the Cortez family. They were from Chihuahua and headed to Torreon. Their appreciation was overflowing to the brothers. They found themselves penned down by the ambush and probably could not have gotten out by themselves.

The brothers told Jesse Cortez they would travel with them until Torreon. They were there by the end of the next day.

Jesse bought them supper at the town's only café. Then they thanked the brothers for saving their lives. The brothers said they would look for them the next time they were in Chihuahua.

After a restful night's sleep, Troy beat his two brothers up. He made coffee. And when Aubrey and Don got up, they had some hard biscuits together and discussed the next few days of travel.

Troy said, "I suppose since we have already been involved in an ambush we might relax and think that possibility is not likely anymore. But I have a feeling that more than one ambush might be a possibility. I think we should be especially careful between here and Matamoros. If we see any likely spots in front of us, we should look for ways to completely avoid the area. Our time will be slowed down some; but it should save us time in the long run, if we avoid trouble."

Aubrey said, "I completely agree. I have been trying to avoid trouble my whole life. This is certainly no time to ignore that rule."

Don said, "With you guys putting out all this wisdom, how could I possibly disagree? Avoidance of trouble is our goal."

Troy said, "I have been looking at the map and it appears that we have made it halfway. I put a mark on the map where I think it is likely we can camp for the night. We can look at that again when we stop for our noon break. But for now, we can get the horses ready and pull out as soon as possible. I am starting to smell saltwater and it is calling my name."

Don laughed and said, "Yeh, I bet you can."

Aubrey said, "I think it is calling my name too. And it keeps saying run, run."

Morning went fast. The road was smooth and flat. It became hilly in the afternoon, and they kept their eyes peeled for likely ambush spots. Fortunately, there were none. They did not worry about that. They knew that their fortunes could change for the bad just as quickly as it did for the good.

Toward the end of the day, the hills got higher and steeper. They crested a hill at one point and saw an area ahead that could mean trouble. Avoiding it seemed like it would be difficult, but also seemed the best course of action.

The brothers left the normal trail and headed north. Quickly, they got into the remnants of the sandy desert that had been to their east since leaving Chihuahua. At this point, the sand was not deep, so crossing it was easy. They kept an eye out to the south where it was visible. The possible ambush site was in the hills. It was not possible to see any evidence of an ambush team; but the decision was a good one anyway.

The trail farther along looked safe enough, so they got back to the trail when they could. Camp was near a spring, south of the main trail. There was no evidence of other caravans or individuals in the area.

Troy slept well. Don and Aubrey slept fitfully because the ocean was coming closer. No matter how relaxed Troy seemed about sailing on the open ocean, they could not feel good about it.

Troy was not as relaxed as he seemed about sailing across the gulf. He knew this was not the best time of year to sail. The possibility of storms was a reality. But, he hoped, if they ran into a storm while on- board a ship, it would not be a bad one. He did not want Aubrey and Don to have an unpleasant trip for their first-time sailing. He was not worried about their safety, only their comfort.

He should have been worried about both.

The largest hurricane in anybody's memory was headed to- ward the gulf. The storm had started in the Atlantic Ocean off the Western Sahara of Africa. It gradually crossed the Atlantic gaining energy, at first dipping down into the Caribbean Sea. It traveled south of the Greater Antilles and turned northwest aiming to cross the Yucatan Peninsula. The Rampy brothers had no idea what was roaring into their path.

The brothers got up the next morning feeling ready to go; but also irritable, for some reason none of them could put their finger on. It was a beautiful day and they made good mileage. They passed by Saltillo late that afternoon, traveling late into the evening. A camp was finally settled into by a spring near the main route.

Weather was beautiful the next day. It made everyone's spir- its rise. They still had a feeling of foreboding that could not be described, but they had not discussed it.

That morning they noticed a possible ambush site up ahead that needed to be avoided. The avoidance took about two extra hours off their trip and they felt good about the effort.

In two more days, they reached Matamoros. It was a small town compared to Chihuahua that seemed to be especially busy. There was movement all over town. Fortunately, there were two ships moored to the dock. That must have been part of the reason the town seemed so busy.

Troy talked to several people on the dock and found out that one ship, the Tampa, was going to be sailing south along the coast when they had enough crew. The other ship, the Norfolk, supposedly had enough crew and should be sailing east along the coast in two days.

The first mate on the Norfolk told Troy the captain was not available that day, but would be back the next. Troy asked him to notify the captain that they would like to book passage for three men and six horses to New Orleans.

Aubrey was able to rent a room for the three of them at one of two hotels in town. He was surprised. With all the people in town, he figured their odds of getting a room were slim to none. But most of the sailors stayed onboard the ship. The other people in town apparently lived there or were camping outside town.

The brothers ate supper in the dining room of the hotel. Just like the streets outside, the dining room was plenty busy. Food there was good too.

After supper the brothers decided to walk around town, check their horses at the hotel stable, and then call it a night.

10 | SAILING FROM MATAMOROS

"Well, I do not believe it. Troy Rampy," said a voice behind the brothers, as they ate breakfast.

Troy jumped up from his table and turned around. His face lit up and he said, "Peter Lamont, what on earth are you doing here? I figured you would make your way back to Boston and never leave again."

The two men hugged each other like two bears wrestling. They were both practically crying by the time they turned loose of each other.

"Peter, these are two of my brothers, Aubrey, and Don. Fellows, this is an old friend, Peter Lamont. We sailed together along the U.S. east coast. Peter, please sit with us. Tell us what you are up to these days."

"I would be glad to, Troy, but I can only stay a few minutes. I have got to get back to my ship. I am captain of the Norfolk. Hopefully, we will sail tomorrow and there are many things to do before then."

Troy looked somewhat in shock. He said, "You are a captain. I cannot believe it. After Juan and I left, I was convinced that you would leave too once you got back close enough to home. What changed your mind? By the way, the three of us and our six horses are hoping to sail to New Orleans with you. If you will have us?"

"I would love to have you on board. We can catch up and I will tell you why I am still sailing. Maybe I had better get to the ship. Come see me at Norfolk when you get there. We can talk some more. It is exciting to see you again and I am so glad you are coming with us as far as New Orleans. Aubrey and Don, it is a pleasure to meet you. I have lots of stories to tell you about Troy and our days sailing together."

"See you soon, Peter," Troy said.

Troy was obviously excited when he turned to his brothers and said, "That is amazing. I thought I might see Peter again someday, but not at a seaport. He was with Juan and I when we went through that terrible storm, I told you about. That seemed like it would be the end of every one's sailing adventure. It will be interesting to see what kept him on a ship.

"He should be an outstanding captain. I was always impressed with how intelligent and strong he was. Juan and I made several good friends aboard ship; but he was the best."

After breakfast, the brothers walked around town and visited a few more shops. Then they headed to the ship.

When they got to the ship, the first mate told them about the ship.

The Norfolk was a Baltimore Clipper. It was 100 feet long and 25 feet wide at the beam, with a carrying capacity of 280 tons. She had been built sometime between 1798 and 1803 in the Baltimore shipyards.

Originally the ship was configured as a cargo ship; but later reconfigured to use as a war ship in the War of 1812. She was never used in the war because of a problem with placing and securing cannons on deck. Before the problem was solved, the war was over. Then the Norfolk was reconfigured to its original cargo setup and re-named. She was named for a port farther down the coast she was intended to sail from.

The Norfolk was a double masted ship. It had the main mast in the rear and the fore mast in the front. It was rigged with stay sails reaching forward from the fore mast and backward from the main mast. In addition to that, both masts were rigged with square sails at the top.

If used in a conflict as a war ship, the Norfolk would have a crew of forty to fifty men and a dozen cannons. As a cargo ship, the Norfolk had a crew of fifteen men including the captain. There would be four men on deck day and night, if they were under sail. At dock there were two guards on deck during the day and four at night.

Captain Lamont came up to the Rampys as they talked to the first mate. He smiled at the brothers and said, "Troy, I am so glad to see you again and glad that you and your brothers will be on board with us as far as New Orleans. Let me show you around."

They started at the front of the ship and looked at the rigging, deck, supplies, tools, and equipment.

"Captain Lamont," Troy said, "I see that you have what seems like an adequate number of fore-and-aft sails to propel the ship, but you have added some square sails on the top of the masts. Is that because of the weight of the cargo you carry?"

"No, not really. That is just intended to give us the opportunity for more speed, if the need arises. And since we are talking about that possibility, I need to mention something.

"Recently I was warned that there have been several sightings in the last month of what people thought might be pirates or privateers. I have never seen them in these waters. However, if a boat unknown to us advances on us, we will run. And those extra sails should give us more speed.

"It is puzzling why they would be attacking ships along this coast. There are certainly no treasure ships that sail this path. And those of us who are regulars here, carry normal types of cargo. That is not generally what a pirate or privateer would be interested in. Afterall, they need to sell whatever they take. And that just makes them cargo haulers themselves.

"I hope if the time comes and the pirates get close enough to shoot at us, you guys could help us with some additional fire power."

"Sure Peter, we would certainly do that. We would not want to stand by and do nothing while we were being attacked."

"Thanks Troy. I appreciate that a great deal."

"I understand that you are planning to push out in the morning. Is that correct?"

"Yes, I hope we can leave about an hour after sunup."

"That should work well for us. My brothers and I will get our horses on board about sunup.

"Let me know if you need help with anything. Don and Aubrey have never sailed before. We are all good workers though. We will help any way we can."

"That would be great Troy. I think it will be fun sailing with you again and your brothers. I hope we have a nice smooth sail and your brothers, and you enjoy it. Have a good day here in Matamoros and I will see you in the morning."

"See you then."

The Rampy brothers spent their day walking around town. It seemed to be a combination port town and a normal inland Mexican town. A dozen or so merchants had shops along the dock and within several streets. There were several cafes scattered around the main town area.

The day went fast and before they knew it, the day was over. The brothers went to sleep early, so they could get their horses and themselves on board around sun-up.

Troy did not sleep well. He was excited about the trip. There was something else that concerned him. He was not quite sure what was eating at him, he finally got up and stirred his brothers too.

They had their horses and equipment over to the ship and loaded by the time the sun came up. Once their personal gear was all onboard, the brothers stayed on deck talking to the deck hands and the captain.

When it was time to push out away from the dock, the first mate, Bob Jameson, was able to set the front fore-and-aft sail in a position to allow them to push the ship away from the deck. This was not always possible. Today it worked perfectly.

Matamoros' dock was on the Rio Grande River instead of the gulf so Captain Lamont sailed the ship down the broad expanse of the river into the Gulf of Mexico. The water here was deep, so hitting a snag or some other object was not likely. Wind and the current pushed the ship along at a good clip.

As the ship approached the gulf, Troy could see where the two bodies of water came together. The water was as smooth as glass, so everyone on board was anticipating a smooth sailing. Of course, that was tempered by the knowledge that weather can change suddenly and the knowledge that there may be pirates between here and New Orleans.

Once the ship was in the open ocean and one of the crew manning the wheel, Captain Lamont started his rounds on the main deck. As he was finishing his rounds he stopped to talk with Troy Rampy.

"Troy, it is so good to see you again, and to be sailing with you also. Tell me what you have been up to for the past five or six years."

Troy said, "Peter, I would be glad to, but I suspect your story is more interesting than mine, so I am looking forward to your story much more than mine.

"Well, even before that big blow we went through, I was looking for something else to do. I had finally decided that owning a store was what I wanted to do. I knew it would allow me to meet many new and interesting people. And it would allow me to learn many things, especially when you consider you need to learn something about everything you sell. A dry goods or hardware store sounded like the best idea, so with that in mind, I decided to quit sailing once we got to New Orleans, if the captain could find enough crew. Thankfully, he was able to find all the crew he needed, so I told him I was not going any farther."

"Troy, I can see you as a dry goods merchant. You always were good with people and had a good head for details."

Troy said, "The first thing I did in New Orleans was to look for a job or other opportunities in selling dry goods or hardware. I found an older man who had a small store. He sold mainly hardware, but also some dry goods. He was interested in selling out and moving back to Virginia where most of his family lived. A local banker was a friend of his and agreed to loan me enough money to buy the store and the merchandise in it. So, suddenly I was a merchant.

"New Orleans was busy and getting busier, so the store did well. There were many people moving into town to settle. And there were people moving north into the interior to settle that area. I was able to quickly pay off the loan and expand the store. I was able to stock the store with about whatever someone would need if they were moving to a new town or moving cross country to a new state."

"Yes Troy, thank goodness for people moving here and there. That keeps ships busy and ship captains employed."

Troy continued, "After a few years, my youngest brother, Bill, came to visit me. He helped with the store, and we had a good time together. The store continued to grow, and we thought about ways to expand again.

"Then one day, Bill and I came up with the idea of trading in Spanish territory. The Mexicans, by that time, were fighting a war for independence with Spain and appeared to be winning. We thought that the Mexican merchants would be needing new trading partners once they separated from Spain.

"Bill had a good strong horse and got two more sturdy pack

horses. He loaded them with a variety of goods and took off for Santa Fe. His idea was to get to know some people there and see if there were people we could trade with. When I left the ship in New Orleans, I knew that Juan Leos was also intending to go back to Santa Fe and start some kind of store or business there. Since then, I had heard that Juan was back in Santa Fe or around there somewhere close. So, I asked Bill to find Juan while he was there.

"He did find him and got to know him and most of the merchants in Santa Fe, from the sound of it. Most of the merchants were related to Juan, as it turned out. Bill went with Juan and some other Santa Fe merchants to a trade fair in Chihuahua. There, he met a lot more merchants and found a woman he wanted to marry. Instead of marrying her, he came back to New Orleans to report the good opportunities he had found in Santa Fe and Chihuahua. By the time Bill got back to New Orleans, our other two brothers had leased their farms in Alabama and come to see what Bill and I were doing. When Bill got back, Don and Aubrey had been with me for about six weeks.

"After Bill told us about the opportunities in Santa Fe, we decided to take several wagons of goods to Santa Fe. I turned my store over to two partners to manage until I got back. Then we got some wagons and loaded them with goods to take on our caravan."

"Wow, Troy, that must have been quite a trip. How on earth did you get there?"

"Peter, that is another long story. I can tell you that later; but now I would like to hear your story about how you became a ship captain. As I recall, after that storm, you were about as ready as I was to seek some other kind of work."

Peter laughed and said, "Yes, I was ready. I think I saw my life flash before my eyes four or five times on that trip. I thought I was a dead man. And I thought all of you were joining me, to wherever it is that sailors go when they die.

"When we survived, I truly was amazed. I did not think I would ever step on another ship again, for any reason, much less to sail on the open ocean. I told myself that once the ship got back to my home port, I would get off and find different work. I meant it too. That storm scared me to death."

Troy said, "So, what got you back into sailing?"

He laughed again and said, "Hang on, Troy, I am eventually going to get there. I got off at New Port and took a job handling cargo. Of course, that kept me in contact with other sailors and boat captains. One day our old captain stopped by to see me. The owner of his ship was buying another ship and had asked his captain for a recommendation. He recommended me because he trusted my work and knew where he could find me.

"They had me ride with the captain on his ship for a couple of weeks. He taught me everything he knew, all the tricks of the trade. Especially how he was able to save the boat in that storm. I felt much more confident after that. And he told me in his twenty years of sailing, that was by far the worst storm he had ever seen.

"That in itself, made me feel more confident about sailing. Just to think the odds of me seeing another storm like that were slim."

"Peter, I am certainly glad you are our captain. It is a pleasure sailing with you again. I hope the sea will be as calm as it is today for our entire trip."

"Troy, you know that is unlikely, but we can always hope."

"Yes, we can. Without hope, what could we do?"

Along with the calm seas, came calm winds, so the ship was certainly not getting off to a fast start. By afternoon the winds did pick up speed and the waves started to form.

The captain had his men work primarily with the fore and aft sails. The ship began to make a good headway. He intended to save the square sails until there was more wind for them to catch. He did not think that would take long.

The afternoon found the ship in even rougher water. The increase in wind continued to push the ship along well. The captain thought the ship would be in the area of Corpus Christi Cove by mid-morning the next day. He did not anticipate stopping there because there was no settlement. It was a good reference point along the coast. They could also stop in the cove if there were any problems.

The Norfolk sailed steadily all night and by 9:00 the next morning they were within a few miles of Corpus Christi.

About thirty minutes later as they passed the cove, the lookout called to notify the captain that another ship was sailing out of the cove in their direction.

As the captain had already planned to do in the event of an unknown boat approaching them, he commanded the boat to be steered to the east. He also asked his first mate to have the square sails hoisted.

The Norfolk had been sailing north along the coast, so this change of direction took them directly away from the other ship.

The sailors on deck immediately adjusted the sails, as they lost wind with the change of tack. The wind blowing from the southeast had filled the sails well as they headed north; but their tack to the east allowed the sails to catch less wind. Of course, the boat following them had the same problem with the wind. That boat appeared to be about two miles behind Norfolk.

Captain Lamont was captaining his ship from near the wheel, but he had another sailor steering it. The wheel was in the rear quarter of the ship.

Troy Rampy came to see the captain and offer his help. "Captain Lamont, please remember that my brothers and I would be glad to help in any way we can. How can you use us?"

The captain smiled tensely and said, "I think we are doing all we can at the minute, Troy, so I do not need you for anything now. If the pirate ship gets close enough for them to fire at us, I would like for you to return fire. I am hoping that we can keep ahead of them, but that may not last long depending upon their weight and sails. From what I can see, it appears they have the same fore and aft sails that we do, but not the square sails. Hopefully, our square sails will keep Norfolk ahead of the pirates."

The Norfolk's race with the other ship lasted an hour or so, with the Norfolk well in the lead. Eventually, the other ship was able to catch enough wind to bring her closer to Norfolk, but still not within rifle range.

The seas began to get rougher and both ships had to maneuver to avoid the biggest of the waves. It had become obvious that a storm was headed toward them from the southeast.

The Rampy brothers made sure their weapons and ammunition were ready and close at hand.

Troy went and talked to Captain Lamont. He got close to the captain and said, "I cannot believe how far the pirate ship has followed us. I would have thought they would give up after forty-five minutes or so. But now they have been following us for a couple of hours. They must be hungry."

"I know. Troy, I am surprised too. I think they must see that they are gradually gaining on us and feel like they will eventually come alongside us. And frankly, they may. What do you think about this storm coming in from the southeast? It reminds me of the big storm we hit while we were still sailing together."

"I agree, Peter. It looks more dangerous than the ship behind us. I have been thinking we should turn south and then eventually southwest to see if we can avoid the biggest part of it."

"That sounds good to me. I am going to make that change gradually, so the other ship does not catch up to us as easily as it would if we made a drastic change. I will have the first mate tell the men what my plan is and then we will execute it gradually."

Captain Lamont called for his first mate and discussed the situation and what he intended to do. He asked the first mate to notify the men on the sails.

Troy was still nearby the captain, so he asked Troy to be ready with his brothers in case there was gunfire exchanged with the pirate ship.

As the Norfolk turned more directly into the southeast wind. but still tacking to the left, the ship picked up speed. The ship sailed in that direction just long enough to see that it was pulling away from the other ship. but slowly. They continued that way for twenty minutes and then turned across the wind to tack to the right of the wind. Holding to that position as long as they could, they stalled at first and then started to pick up speed again.

The pirate ship began to draw close to Norfolk because it made the maneuver more smoothly. Finally, it appeared there might be a gun battle after all.

When the ships got within fifty yards of each other, rifle fire came from the other ship. Troy, his brothers, and three other sailors returned fire.

Trying to fire a rifle at a moving target from a moving ship going over five-to-seven-foot swells was difficult to impossible; but both sides kept firing for thirty minutes.

Toward the end of the firing, the Norfolk's fighters started firing toward the steering wheel on the boat to see if they could disrupt the steering. That disruption worked and caused the other ship to make a radical movement that caused them to lose the wind in their sales. By the time they caught the wind again, the Norfolk was well ahead and never to be caught again.

By the time the fighting was over, Captain Lamont decided they were in a dangerous situation. An enormous storm was barreling toward them.

Captain Lamont thought the best course of action would be running as fast as they could to the southwest. That may let them get out of the way of the storm, or at least the worst part of the storm. He had no idea what the odds were for their survival.

The pirate ship turned toward the coast and hoped the storm would push them back to where they came from. The captain of that ship probably felt he had a seventy-five percent chance of survival.

11 | THROUGH THE STORM

Captain Lamont would have turned back to the southwest sooner if he had not been distracted by the pirate ship. He feared he may have waited too long to get away from the storm.

With smoother seas the Norfolk's run to the southwest might have been quicker and safer; but that was far from the conditions they found themselves in now. The swells continued to grow with some occasional waves being eight feet or more. The Norfolk needed to hit these waves head-on to keep from getting rolled. They needed to climb over the waves, not be pushed over by the wave.

Along with the high seas came more wind. The wind was strong and erratic. It was especially difficult to keep the sails filled with wind when one minute it was blowing and then it was not blowing. And then it would be completely wild. Captain Lamont was afraid the Norfolk would lose a mast or a sail or both. The ship would practically jump out of the water on the tallest waves. Then it would hit the valley between two waves with a boom that shook the entire ship. After that, climbing the next wave seemed like scaling a mountain. Sometimes the Norfolk would stall halfway up, like it was about to fall. Fortunately, the wind would catch in the sails just in time to push the ship over the top of the wave.

Troy found Captain Lamont by the wheel. He was helping a sailor with the job of steering. The high waves had made steering incredibly difficult.

The captain said, "What do you think, Troy? Is this storm as bad as the last one you went through together?"

"Not yet. As I recall, that one lasted several days. I am hoping we will be able to get out of this one before it carries us to the coast."

"My feelings exactly. If we can get to the edge of this storm, we will be alright.

"That ship full of pirates is in trouble. This storm will carry them to the shore and break them up in a thousand pieces. Hey, I appreciate you and your brothers helping my men keep the pirates away, long enough that the situation changed for our benefit."

"We were glad to do it. And anything else we can help with, just let us know."

"I certainly will, Troy."

The Norfolk continued to sail to the southwest. It rolled over high waves for hours. Then finally the waves started to get smaller and then wind decreased in its violence. It was never clear where the ship finally got clear of the body of the storm. The wind and the waves were still big enough to cause problems and the captain and his sailors still had difficulty steering the ship into the evening hours.

Sailors tried to get a few hours of sleep when they could; but most of the time, they were alert and watching for problems with the masts or sails.

When the sun came up the next morning, the captain and his first mate went over the ship from top to bottom, looking for damage. Captain Lamont was amazed there was so little damage. Oh, there was damage, but not what he thought there might be. The sails were all ripped and torn, but none of them was missing. The masts held together also.

Captain Lamont knew that if they had gotten caught by the worst of the storm, nobody would be alive to do this evaluation today. The Norfolk and its crew would be at the bottom of the gulf.

Troy and his brothers were on the bow of the ship looking out to sea. They all looked miserable and disheveled. Aubrey and Don both had a slightly green cast to their skin.

Don said, "Troy, I gather that this past twenty-four hours was not what you were used to during your sailing days?"

Troy laughed boisterously and finally said, "No, that was not typical by any stretch of the imagination. That was probably the second worst time at sea that I have ever had. The last storm that I went through, before I quit sailing, was worse. But it was only worse because we got caught in the middle of it. That storm pushed us for days. This storm may have been bigger, but we were able to get to the edge of it and away from the main body.

"So how did you guys do during the storm? Oh, by the way, Captain Lamont told me thanks for our work with his men to keep the pirates away from the ship. He said he really appreciated our work."

Aubrey said, "Troy, despite you telling us we would not likely get in a storm, and if we did it probably would not be a bad storm, I think we did alright. Oh, I got sick six of eight times, but I am alright now."

"I would have to say about the same, Troy," added Don. "I am feeling much better. I may have thrown up a dozen times or so, but once it was over, I began to feel much better. Not that I want to be a sailor or anything, but I am okay sailing now."

Troy chuckled and said, "Well, good I was a little worried you guys would hate me for bringing you on this adventure. I am certainly glad we survived, and your overall experience was not awful."

Don said, "I did not say that it was not awful. It was awful. but I am just much better now."

Troy and Aubrey laughed at Don's comment.

"I think we should go talk to Captain Lamont and see what he is thinking. And see where he thinks we are."

The brothers found the captain back by the wheel. He was working on it with the sailor who had been doing most of the steering the day before.

"Hi, Troy," said the captain. "How are you and your brothers doing on this beautiful day?"

"We are doing fine. How are you doing and how is the ship and your crew?"

"I am doing amazingly well considering the past twenty-four hours. The ship is a different story. Oh, it is not too bad, but there is a lot of work that needs to be done. I am glad we ran away from the storm when we did. I hate to think what the inside of that storm would have been like.

"I thought our steering problem yesterday was just the high seas, but it is not any better. We need to stop in a cove somewhere to have a diver look at the rudder. And while we are there, it would also be good to patch the sails and lines. Thank goodness the masts are still in good shape. It is almost unbeliev-able to go through a storm like that, without losing a mast and several sails.

"We should be getting close to the Mexico coast. I am hop-ing to find a cove where we can put in for a few days. Then, when we get everything patched up, I can point Norfolk toward Houston. I do not think there would be any reason to stop at ports west of there. Likely, nothing would be left at those ports."

Norfolk soon found the Mexican coast and the search for a quiet cove began. About two hours later, a pleasant cove was found, and the Norfolk anchored in it.

Captain Lamont set his sailors to work taking down damaged sails, which was most of them, and repairing them. Most of the repairs were just patches, but there were a few small sails that needed to be replaced.

One sailor, that was an excellent swimmer, was sent under the boat to look at the rudder. It was too late in the day for the swimmer to see the rudder well enough to figure out the problem. It was thought that tomorrow when the sun was high, the underwater visibility would be better.

After the good light was gone for the day, everyone on board was shuttled to the beach by the ship's supple boat. A fire was built, and everyone sat and enjoyed food, peaceful rest, and talked for a few hours.

"Captain Lamont," Troy said, "this is a unique surprise. It is what back home they would call a picnic."

He laughed and said, "I just thought we all could use a little rest, after the stress of that blow."

"I agree. This is great."

"It will certainly be interesting to see what tomorrow brings."

Troy said, "I cannot say that my brothers have enjoyed their sailing trip, so far. But they certainly have learned a lot.

"What do you suppose is wrong with the rudder and how can it be fixed?"

"Good question, Troy. Since it still works somewhat, I would be willing to bet it is not broken. I think something got under the boat and wedged itself in the rudder mechanism. If that is the case, it should not be difficult to fix. However, if it is bent or broken, it will be a much bigger problem."

Troy said, "Do you remember that time we put the ship in at Boston and were having somewhat the same problem. It turned out to be easy to fix and I am hoping this is the same way."

Captain Lamont asked his first mate to get the men headed back toward the boat for the night. There was a little rum being passed around and he wanted the men to get back to the ship before there were any problems.

The next day was a beautiful day and gave everyone hope they could soon finish the repairs and get Norfolk headed toward Houston.

Those working on the sail got a mighty good start underway. Most of the patchable sails had been repaired. The others were close to being finished.

By noon, the swimmer, Jacob, slid under the boat again. Captain Lamont was beginning to worry something had gone wrong when his head popped out of the water. He said that an object, like a log, was wedged into the steering mechanism. He thought with a few more dives he could get it dislodged.

Jacob took a small metal bar under the water with him on the next dive. When he came up, he said he had made progress on dislodging the object.

He had spent a lot of effort on the attempt and needed to rest before he tried again.

After an hour, Jacob grabbed his prybar and went down for another attempt. He had barely gotten under the water when Don said, "What is that over there?" He pointed toward shore where a large fin stuck up out of the water, moving slowly back and forth.

Troy said, "Oh no, that is a shark, and they are extremely dangerous to swimmers. We need to get Jacob out of the water, but I have no idea how."

Captain Lamont was standing nearby. He said, "I have an idea how we might alert him."

He had the first mate find a hammer and pound on the wheel.

About twenty seconds later, Jacob popped up and asked if there was something wrong. He saw the shark and quickly got out of the water.

By that time, the entire crew was watching for sharks. Several more were sighted within a hundred feet or so of the boat.

Jacob said to Captain Lamont, "Well, I think that is probably all the swimming for today or at least for a while. I almost had the object removed. One more trip down should do it; but I do think we should wait until the sharks leave."

The captain said, "Absolutely. We cannot afford to have you injured. I think you are our only good swimmer. Without you, we would be in trouble."

The sharks stayed in the area for the rest of the day, so it was decided to spend the night and try again as soon as the sharks left.

Next morning the sharks were still around. In fact, a fourth one had joined them.

Jacob went to the captain with an idea. He said, "Captain, if we spin the wheel back and forth enough, it may dislodge the object. It was almost loose the last time I was down there."

The captain and first mate worked on the wheel. At first, it still seemed stiff to turn, but then suddenly began to spin freely. They decided Jacob should go down one more time to check the rudder before they leave.

Just when it looked like the sharks would never leave, they disappeared. It was early in the afternoon. The crew looked carefully for thirty minutes and no more were spotted.

Jacob got in the water one more time, without the bar, and went under. A minute later, he was up and gave the captain a thumbs up signal.

Captain Lamont decided they would spend one more night in the cove and leave at first light.

By sun-up the Norfolk was just beginning to ease out of the cove. The wind was light, but should increase soon.

The ship was pointed to the northeast, toward the northern coast of the gulf. All the sails were set, including the square sails. The prevailing winds, as usual, were coming out of the southwest. That should make for a good day.

Mid-morning Troy was talking to his brothers on deck. He said, "Guys, how are you feeling about your first ocean voyage now?"

Don said, "Honestly Troy, considering that you have told us that the storm we went through will probably be the worst storm we ever see, and considering that we survived, I would say that this is a mighty fine voyage." That made them all laugh.

"Really, Troy, it has been interesting and educational. I have learned how the rigging on a sailing ship works. I have learned how to repair sails and I have learned how to steer a sailing ship. Of course, I have no idea how the captain can determine where they are and where they are going. But other than that, sailing seems like an interesting profession. I enjoyed it for a while, but it has its ups and its downs. I just got tired of the downs. How about you, Aubrey? Are you ready to sail back to Matamoros?"

"Well, I could do it. Here we have only been on the water a week and have already ridden out a hurricane. Seems like an easy way to travel. Truth be told, it is fast, if we can stay away from storms. Why do you ask, Troy? Are you trying to decide if we should go back to Albuquerque the way we came? Or are you thinking about going back through St. Louis and cross country like before?"

"Aubrey, you are exactly right. I am trying to decide how we should go back to Albuquerque. Either way will be expensive. If we go part of the way back by ship, it will probably be faster, but it will cost more. And there is no guarantee that it will be faster. If we go back by cargo wagon, we will need more manpower. Either way has its own risks and problems.

"One thing I have been thinking about is following Bill's first route to Santa Fe. Remember, he left from New Orleans and found his way to the Red River. He followed that three quarters of the way. Once he got to the beginnings of the Red River, he kept going west and finally got into the mountains near Santa Fe.

"Since I am wanting to take wagon loads of equipment to my new store, I probably should take it from my business partner's store. That would make our separation easier, and it might be better in general. It would be fun to go to St. Louis again and buy things from our friends there; but it would take far longer and be more difficult in the long run.

"So, I guess I am thinking either Bill's original route or the reverse of the way we are going now."

Aubrey said, "That sounds good to me. Either of those ways should be quicker than going through St. Louis, as much fun as that would be. Bill talked so much about his solo ride from New Orleans to Santa Fe and how pretty, exciting, and interesting it was. I think I would like to go that way. And it surely is much quicker than through St. Louis. What do you think, Don?"

"I certainly agree with you two on either the sea route or Bill's original route. Although, some strange thing in me would like to go through St. Louis, just so I could see where I was almost killed. But I am not suggesting that. I really like the idea of Bill's original route the most. It would be exciting to see it and eventually to tell Bill we did it. Then we could all reminisce about it. So, I would vote for that route."

Troy said, "Thanks for those comments, guys. I am certainly inclined to Bill's route, too; but we should wait until we get to New Orleans to make the final decision. I cannot see much changing between here and there.

The Norfolk continued to sail smoothly on the prevailing winds that pushed them toward the distant coast. It seemed almost like the storm had blown away any problems in their path and was giving them a smooth and safe sail. It was likely that the first port they got close to would be at Galveston. There was not an official port at Galveston yet; but there was enough of a dock that a ship can load and unload.

Troy and his brothers had late lunch with Captain Lamont that afternoon.

"Peter, how is everything going? This is truly a beautiful day."

"Yes, it certainly is beautiful, Troy. We could not ask for a better day. The water is smooth, and the prevailing winds are taking us where we want to go. We are headed toward Galveston, although I am tempted to go a little farther west to see what the damage is along the coast. I am assuming there is lots of damage. There are probably no ports along there where we could stop anyway. In fact, I do think we will go a little farther west to see what damage we can see. We should report that to the ports we stop at."

Captain Lamont changed the Norfolk's course to take it along the worst of the damage according to his calculations. The following day they should be close to the area where the storm hit the hardest.

The Norfolk sailed on to the north with smooth seas and good wind behind them. The Rampy brothers worked with their gear and horses. Gear had been rolled around the hold, where it was kept, but not damaged. Being mainly soft gear, it was difficult to damage. The horses had been shaken and bruised badly, but had survived without any broken legs. They had been cinched up tightly in their small stalls before the storm hit. It remained to be seen how they would be once Norfolk got to land.

By sun-up the next morning, the ship was still a couple of hours from the coast. All the men on board assumed they would be seeing evidence of the storm soon. As it turned out, they were right. Here and there was debris floating in the water.

As the Norfolk got within sight of land, it became obvious the captain had gotten his calculations right concerning where the storm would have hit land. Up and down the coast was debris from damaged trees and other plants. There occasionally was evidence of where a structure was destroyed; but not too many people lived along the coast. Wreckage of a few small boats was also seen.

About fifteen miles up the coast they were still seeing wreckage from the storm. At an area where there were small dunes, the captain saw what he assumed was the ship that had chased them out to sea. It had been pushed about a quarter mile up onto shore. It lay on its side, demolished. No evidence was apparent of survivors in the area, so the Norfolk sailed on. Wreckage became less apparent after that.

The captain set sail for Galveston which was two to three more days east.

No further damage was seen, from their vantage point about a mile off the coast. The Norfolk sailed through the rest of that day and into the next afternoon, with a strong tailwind. Then the winds changed direction and started coming out of the south. The skies darkened and the captain and crew began to worry.

If another hurricane was brewing, Norfolk would have difficulty avoiding it. They were far too close to shore to maneuver out of the path of any damage. Sailing on was the only alternative and praying that the storm would not develop the way it appeared it might.

Captain Lamont continued toward Galveston. His calculations indicated they should reach the port by noon the next day if they survived this coming storm.

The captain asked his crew, that were not busy with duty on the sail lines, to secure everything they could. The Rampy brothers looked after their gear and the horses. The horses had already survived the big storm, so Troy thought they would survive this one. He felt the odds of having a second hurricane this quick after another one were slim. He had never heard of that happening.

Troy stopped by to talk to Captain Lamont about the storm. He found him near the wheel.

"Peter, do you think this storm will develop into a bad one?"

He smiled and said, "No, Troy, I do not think it will be serious; but it is a good reminder for us to be careful. I think we will get some rain and wind, but not enough to do any damage. I am moving farther away from the coast in case the wind would want to push us on shore. My calculations have us getting to

Galveston by early tomorrow afternoon. I hope that is correct. And I hope I am correct about this storm."

"I hope your calculations are right. I agree with you about the storm, I have never seen a big storm follow another one this quick. I am like you, just thinking that there will be rain and wind."

The storm continued to develop, but it only provided heavy rain and lots of wind. By midnight it was finished.

Later that morning the sun came up on a beautiful day. By early afternoon they were close to docking at Galveston. The Norfolk sailed to the north side of the island where the port was. There was a great deal of excitement because of the Norfolk coming into port.

The Norfolk's cargo holds held 1,100 pounds of cargo for businesses in Galveston. The word of a ship in port would spread across the small town quickly. Any businessman awaiting cargo or needing to ship cargo would be there soon.

Once the ship was secured to the dock, there were already several men there wanting to talk to the captain. The sailors would need to stay on board until any cargo was handled.

The Rampy brothers disembarked after talking to the captain. He told them they would spend the night at the port and then sail in the morning.

Market Street and Mechanic Street made up the retail in town, so the brothers walked up and down the street to see what was there. Galveston was the most prominent port west of New Orleans, so the merchants here were the competition of Troy's store.

Troy enjoyed his time walking in and out of the stores and talking to the proprietors. You could buy many items here that also were available in New Orleans; but his store and fellow merchants had a definite advantage.

As Troy walked into a clothing store, someone called to him, "Troy, what are you doing here?"

"Matt Carmichael, it is good to see you. My story is way too long. Tell me what you are doing here."

"I live here now. My wife and I own this clothing store. We have been here three years and have one daughter, Virginia, who is one year old.

"So, tell me your long story. I have time to listen. I usually do not have many customers at this time of day."

"Matt, let me introduce my brothers Aubrey and Don to you. Guys this is Matt Carmichael. He is a friend from New Orleans."

Matt said, "Aubrey and Don, it is nice to meet you. Troy and I had businesses close together in New Orleans.

"So, Troy, please go on with your story."

Troy told him the story of Bill going to Santa Fe and Chihuahua and meeting Frances. He continued with Troy's trip with Don, Aubrey and friends to Santa Fe and Albuquerque.

"I fell in love with the town of Albuquerque and have decided I will move my business operation there. I hope to sell my interest in the store to my partners in New Orleans. Then I intend to take some of my share in goods and haul them back to Albuquerque for my new store."

"Wow, Troy, that is quite a story. I do not know anything about Albuquerque; but I have heard of it."

"It is a busy town with a big future from what I can see. I am excited to get back and start my operations there. Matt, how do you like things here?"

"It is a very pleasant place to live. My wife and I like it here a great deal. We will probably make our future here. So, if you guys ever get back to Galveston, please look us up. Troy, it is great to see you again."

"Matt, it is great to see you as well. Take care."

Troy and his brothers continued their walk down the street. They found a nice café for supper, walked a little more, and then went back to the ship to care for their horses and gear.

The next morning when the ship was supposed to sail, they

were still waiting for some cargo. It had not arrived. The captain received a note, by way of a courier, that it should be there by noon.

Rather than leave in the mid-afternoon, Captain Lamont decided they would not sail until the next morning. He released most of the sailors to go ashore, but kept a few to help with the incoming cargo.

The Rampy brothers went ashore again and saw the rest of the town.

Galveston seemed to be a growing town. It was in a good location. There were no other ports between it and New Orleans, but that was starting to change. There had been several attempts at starting a port in other areas; but all had been unsuccessful, so far.

The Island upon which Galveston sat, was at the front of a large bay. There apparently had been some attempts to start towns at different places around the bay, but there was nothing significant yet. Troy thought that anywhere around the bay would be a good location in the future.

Rain started early in the afternoon, so most of the crew and the Rampy brothers headed back for the ship. They were all hoping this would not be a bad storm that might prevent the Norfolk from sailing in the morning.

Thankfully, the storm did not last long, and the Norfolk sailed in the morning shortly after it got light. New Orleans would be the next port. So long as the weather did not interfere, they should be there in four days.

After the brothers made sure their horses were in good shape and had enough feed and water, they spent some time by the rail talking and reminiscing.

"Troy," Aubrey said. "What do you intend to do when we get back to New Orleans?"

"Of course, I will go to the store first and talk to my partners. I have not talked to them in almost a year. They may think that

I have died. Who knows. They may have sold the store, split the money two ways, and headed back to New England. I hope that is not the case. If it is, I will be starting over. A more likely scenario would be me talking them into buying me out with merchandise. Then we can take that merchandise back to Albuquerque and start the new store. What are you guys thinking now? Are you still intending to go back to Albuquerque with me?"

"Yes, I am," said Don. "How about you, Aubrey?"

"I am too. Or at least, I do not have any other plans currently." He laughed.

"Troy," Don said, "What got you interested in New Orleans in the first place? And what got you interested in dry goods?"

"That is a good question, Don. I know we have talked about this before; but it is good to remind myself from time to time, why I started here.

"I like the location in New Orleans. It is central to the southern United States and central to the Gulf of Mexico. And I feel that location is so seriously important if you want to be a retailer. Of course, that is the same thing I like about Albuquerque. Its location is perfect. Now that the war is over and Mexico is in control of her own destiny, merchants will be flowing over that entire part of the World. And, to me, Albuquerque looks like the center of everything. There may be other areas up north that would also be as good as Albuquerque; but I have never seen them and do not know where they are. And with all those huge mountains running north from Santa Fe, anyone traveling across the country would have to be concerned about the difficulty of going west. I have not traveled west from Albuquerque; but, from everything I have learned, it is not nearly as difficult as farther north.

"Don, you also asked me what stirred my interest in dry goods. I am sure that working on a ship that was hauling dry goods from place to place got me interested in that kind of business. I could see that there was a large need for a wide variety of items. Having my own store looked like a good business and a way to settle down somewhere.

"After getting started in New Orleans, I assumed I was settled down for good. Albuquerque convinced me to change locations, but not what I wanted to do. I cannot wait to get back there and get started."

Aubrey chuckled and said, "I do not suppose a certain woman in Albuquerque makes it seem more attractive than it really is?"

"No, Aubrey. Believe it or not, I have given that question a lot of thought and the answer was not made because of my feelings for Justine. I think Justine is a beautiful and intelligent woman, but I am not going back to Albuquerque for her. I was thinking about moving to Albuquerque before I met Justine. The final decision was probably made after I got to know her; but I think the decision would have been the same.

"I would have to admit now that my feelings for Justine are what they are, I am getting anxious to get back there as soon as we can. So, I do not intend to linger in New Orleans any longer than necessary. I intend to get things finalized with my partners and the bank."

"Good for you, Troy," said Don. "I am glad that you will be settling down with a wife. That is probably something Aubrey and I need to do, now that Bill is married, and you likely will be married soon. I cannot imagine that we are even old enough to get married."

"I think we should talk about something different," said Aubrey. "Troy, would you tell us about the port of New Orleans? What is it like? Is it on the ocean or in a bay?"

"The Port of New Orleans is on the Mississippi River. Ships from the gulf must follow, as best they can, the river channel. It curves through what is called the delta. The delta is an area where the dirt brought down the river by the current is deposited. Negotiating the river is not too difficult in the daytime; but I would not want to do it at night.

"You will see when we get there. It is extremely interesting. That is probably all I know about the port of New Orleans. But you two have been there before and it really was not that long ago. We will have a good time. I do not want to stay here more than two weeks."

"I think we should check the horses and then get some sleep."

The next morning the Rampy brothers woke to a beautiful cloud filled, but windy day. Prevailing wind out of the southwest filled all the ship's sails. The ship sailed easily on smooth seas for most of the day. If tomorrow was like this day, by the end of the day Norfolk would be near New Orleans.

The sun rose the next day on another beautiful day. Again, the wind was strong and the seas smooth. By mid-afternoon the Norfolk approached the delta. With luck, Captain Lamont hoped that he and his men would have the Norfolk docked at the port of New Orleans soon.

12 | NEW ORLEANS

Troy and his brothers were on the bow of the Norfolk as it approached the dock at New Orleans. They had been enjoying the approach to the city through the delta. It was fascinating, watching the ship follow the river channel. The Mississippi was incredibly wide and powerful. The amount of land it had carried to the delta was unbelievable.

The brothers had no idea where the Mississippi started; but they knew it must have flowed a long way to have brought so much soil to the delta. Even Troy had never seen anything like it.

As the ship was getting closer to the dock, the brothers stood still watching the city come into view. It really did seem to change into a city while they were gone.

Aubrey looked over at Troy and saw a tear running down his cheek. He said, "Troy, I see you get emotional on getting home to New Orleans. Maybe you are not ready to leave here and move to Albuquerque?"

Troy laughed and said, "I am surprisingly emotional, but I do not think it is about my love for the city. I have been thinking about the business I left behind here, hoping that it is still running, and my partners are doing well. They were both friends of mine by the time I left for Santa Fe. I am looking forward to seeing them and hearing their stories about the past year."

As the Norfolk eased up to the dock, several men helped tie the ship to two moorings.

Troy and his brothers had their gear ready to leave the ship, except for getting the horses saddled.

Once they had the horses and their gear ready to go, the brothers moved the horses off the ship. When the horses were secured at the nearby stable, they found Captain Lamont.

Troy said, "Peter, it has been a pleasure sailing with you again. I hope that we see you again someday. Thank you for getting us here safely. And considering what we went through, I know that was no small task. My intent is to move my operation to Albuquerque, so we will not be here any longer than a few weeks. I am not sure how I intend to get back to Albuquerque. If we decide to go by ship, we will be seeing you. However, there is a very good chance that we will go by horse and wagon, in which case I will probably not see you again."

"Troy, my crew, and I will be taking the Norfolk to Baltimore before we turn around, so I likely will not see you again. But I just wanted you to know what a pleasure it was to have you and your brothers on board. Your friendship has meant a lot to me over the years, and I hope I do see you again. I wanted you to know that you and your brothers helped us a great deal on this sailing. If not for the three of you, that pirate vessel might have caught us and done great damage."

Troy and captain Lamont hugged each other and said goodbye. The Rampy brothers headed toward their horses. Their first stop would be Troy's store.

On the way to the store, it was obvious that New Orleans had grown in the past year. Several new stores, restaurants and repair shops dotted the street as they rode along. Troy thought that, in some ways, it almost appeared to be a different town.

When they got to Troy's store, it looked busy. Troy was certainly glad to see that.

As they entered the store, they identified Troy's partner, Albert McClean, and several other sales personnel. They were all working with customers.

The store looked like it did when Troy left for Santa Fe; but there were many displays that had been rearranged. Troy was pleased with how it looked.

The brothers moved toward Albert. As he looked up from his paperwork and saw who it was, he hung his head and walked toward them.

As Albert reached Troy, it appeared that he had tears in his eyes. Albert said, "Troy, I am so glad to see you. Ralph has been seriously injured and may not live. I have been worried sick about how to run this place without him."

Ralph was the other partner. He ran the manufacturing operation.

Troy asked, "What happened?"

"He was in the shop three days ago working on a tall ladder. One of the other employees moved something that caused a stack of poles to start rolling. Two of the poles rolled into the ladder. The impact did not knock over the ladder; but it was strong enough to make Ralph fall. He could not catch himself and hit the ground on his back. One of the employees stayed with Ralph while another one came to get me. I told him to ride to get the local doctor as soon as possible. I ran out to the shop. When I got to the shop, Ralph was breathing; but not moving.

"The doctor got here in just minutes. There was nothing he could do except keep Ralph comfortable. He said he had a serious concussion and maybe a fractured skull. Apparently, if his brain is bleeding inside, he probably will not live.

"Ralph is at the doctor's office now and has not moved or woken up since the accident. If he wakes up, he might be alright. But, if he does not wake up in a few days, he likely will not survive.

"Troy, this has me scared to death. I do not know if I could run the store without Ralph. I am so glad you came back when you did. Ralph and I have our different parts of the operation. I do not know how to run the manufacturing operation. Plus, when it came to management situations, we made decisions together. Would you like to go to the doctor's office and see Ralph?"

Troy said, "Yes, let's go see him."

Albert and the three brothers got to the doctor's office in about ten minutes. The doctor led them into his spare bedroom. Ralph lay flat on the bed without moving. There was a gray cast to his skin. He looked like he was already dead.

The doctor checked his pulse. It was weak.

Don said, "After I had my wagon accident on the way to Santa Fe, did I look like this?"

Aubrey said, "No, you never looked that gray. Ralph looks like he has already passed."

Troy said, "Doc, how long do you think he can live like this? What is the chance of him recovering?"

The doctor said, "Troy, it is difficult to tell what chance he might have of recovery. But I would say his chances are slim."

"Well, Doc, please keep Ralph as comfortable as you can and do anything you think might help. Please let me know if there is anything I can do."

The doctor said, "I will, Troy."

Troy suggested they go to supper, since it was past time for the store to close. Albert said the employees he left at the store would close the store. Supper was at a restaurant near the doctor's office.

As they waited for supper, Troy outlined his plan to Albert.

"Albert, when we got to Santa Fe, I loved the place. It is a beautiful town in the mountains. The town folk there were all especially nice. My brother, Bill, married a young lady from Chihuahua. It is about six hundred miles south of Santa Fe. About sixty miles south of Santa Fe there is a city named Albuquerque. I am especially drawn to that town. In fact, I have decided to sell you my portion of this operation and move there."

Troy could see the shocked look on Albert's face, so he added, "I was thinking that I would take my payment in goods that I could take back to Albuquerque for my new store. Albert, you, and I can go through your inventory and pick goods that you are overstocked with already. That way it should not put you in a bind."

Troy continued, "But, Albert, with Ralph in such bad condition, we should not do anything until we see what is going to happen. If Ralph starts to recover, we will wait for him to completely recover and then we will move forward with the break-up. If Ralph does not recover, Albert, you and I will work out an agreement that leaves you as owner of the store."

"Wow, Troy, that is a shock. I had no idea three days ago that my life would change so much. You know that I trust you. So, I am willing to move forward with anything you want to do."

Troy said, "For right now, I guess we just need to wait on Ralph and see what his body wants to do. Then we can make decisions after that."

The Rampy brothers spent the night in the hotel. Troy assumed his house was not in shape to stay in for the night. They would look at the house tomorrow.

The three brothers plus Albert had breakfast together in the hotel. Albert seemed much more relaxed after having some time to think about the change Troy was wanting to make in the store.

Albert said, "Troy, I am curious about your trip to Santa Fe with your brothers. How did that go? I am not asking for the whole story. I know we do not have time for that. But I would love to hear the outline of the story."

Troy laughed and said, "I am glad you do not want the entire story. I do not think I could remember everything. Things did go well, except that along the way there was an accident and Don was injured badly. Like Ralph, he lay in a coma for days and we thought he would die. We kept him comfortable in the back of a wagon. After about ten days, he woke up. It still took a little time before he was himself again. He did recover completely. I am certainly hoping that will happen to Ralph."

"In my case," said Don, "I think it was a miracle. We need to pray for Ralph to have a miracle too."

Troy said, "Hey, I think we should go see how Ralph is doing this morning. Then for lunch I will tell you about our adventure to Santa Fe, Albuquerque, and Chihuahua."

Albert said, "Sounds good to me. I am ready to go."

The four of them went to the doctor's office. Albert knocked on the front door. Dr. Taylor answered the door with a concerned look on his face. He said, "Hi. Albert." Then he saw Troy and said, "Hi Troy."

Albert said, "Hi Doc. We were wanting to check on Ralph. Is he doing any better today?"

"No, unfortunately not. I was just checking on him and he seems to be gradually getting worse. I was hoping that it would be the other way around. His pulse was strong at first, after the accident; but now it is getting weaker.

"I will keep him as comfortable as I can. At this point, the best thing we can do for him is pray that God will bring him back to us."

"Doc, do you think he can hear us when we talk to him?" Troy asked.

"I am not sure, Troy. He might be able to hear us. I have not ever read anything about that, although I have heard people suggest it is possible."

Troy walked over to Ralph's bedside, put his hand on his shoulder, and began to talk to him. He said, "Ralph, this is Troy Rampy. My brothers, Aubrey, and Don, have just gotten back here from Santa Fe. Albert told us about the accident. We do not know if you can hear us; but, just in case it is possible, I wanted to tell you a few things.

"I have enjoyed being your partner and I am sorry that I was not here with you and Albert this past year. I appreciate the work that you two have done in keeping the store together. I can tell from looking at the store and shop, that you have both done a great job. We certainly hope that you get over your injury and get back to us. We will be checking in on you each day until you are better. Doc says he will keep you as comfortable as he can.

"Ralph, I just want to say a prayer before we leave; but we will be back tomorrow. Dear God, I just want to pray for Ralph. I pray that you will help him get well. I pray that you will comfort him from now on. And I pray that your will is done in Ralph's life and health. Lord, in your name I pray. Amen."

Troy patted Ralph's shoulder again, as did Aubrey, Don, and Albert.

Then all of them went out into the front room of Doc's office. He said, "I will do everything I can and keep him comfortable."

"Thanks Doc," all of them said.

Troy said, "We will see you tomorrow."

Albert said, "Thanks again, Doc."

Albert went back to the store. Troy and his brothers decided they would walk around town. The four of them agreed they would get together for lunch at the hotel.

Troy and his brothers walked around all eight of the blocks that make up his business neighborhood and visited his old friends. They went into a clothing store, an animal feed store, and an implement dealer. There were two cafes in the area and another that appeared to be starting. There was also an attorney's office and an apothecary.

It was just about 1:00 pm, when they met Albert for lunch. He ordered for the three Rampy brothers. That was fine with them because they would eat about anything. And besides, they were not familiar with all the dishes on the menu. Albert said the restaurant was related to the French in town, but different.

Troy said, "Albert, you wanted to know about our trip to Santa Fe. I will tell you what I can remember. Don and Aubrey can fill in the holes. Of course, I will try not to bore you to death with everything.

Troy explained to Albert how they had gone by steamboat to St. Louis with the intention of riding up the Missouri River aways from there. In St. Louis they saw both the Elliotts and the Russells, who Albert knew as fellow merchants. They told them about their trip and the goods they intended to take. Several of them went on the journey to Santa Fe and took wagon loads of their own merchandise along. He explained how they rode the steamboat until the Missouri was joined by the Kansas River. There they unloaded their wagons and animals. Then they went west until they hit the Arkansas River and followed it to Colorado and then another river down into Santa Fe.

Albert said, "Wow, that sounds like a rugged journey."

Troy said, "It certainly had its rough moments; but it was a trip to remember that is for sure. Maybe you remember that our brother Bill was rushing back to Chihuahua to see a girl he wanted to marry? Her name was Frances. And believe it or not, when we got to Santa Fe, Frances was there with her family watching her brother be installed as a priest. The brother talked Bill and Frances into getting married that day. It was the biggest wedding party I had ever seen. After a few more days celebrating their marriage, Bill and Frances headed to Chihuahua with her family."

Albert asked, "How did the sale of your merchandise go?"

Troy continued, "We sold our goods unbelievably quickly, so when Bill's new family took off for Chihuahua, we went with them. The first big town on the trip was Albuquerque. It was nice and looked prosperous, so we wanted to stay and check it out. My intention was to spend some time there and go on to

Chihuahua. Bill's family has lots of family in Albuquerque also, so they stayed there about a week. When they left, I really was not ready to go. By the time we decided to leave, I had gotten especially interested in starting a store there."

Don interjected, "What he really means is that he had gotten especially interested in a beautiful young lady there."

"In all honesty, Albert, I had gotten interested in the town before I got interested in Justine."

"Justine?" Albert questioned. "My mother's name was Justine. She was lovely. I bet your Justine is lovely also, Troy."

"And Albert, that was our trip to Santa Fe," said Troy. "Oh, there is also the story of us going to Chihuahua to see Bill and Frances. And the story of sailing through a hurricane on the way back to New Orleans. But we should certainly leave that for another day."

"Sounds like some trip, Troy."

"It was Albert," said Aubrey. "It really was. And now we need to go back again to take merchandise to Troy's store." He laughed with somewhat of a grimace on his face. "It is a long way out there."

"When we go back this time, Aubrey, I am thinking of a new route," said Troy. "One that we have never been on, so at least it will be new. And hopefully it will be quicker."

"That is interesting, Troy," said Don. "What route are you thinking about?"

"Did either of you guys ever talk to Bill about his route when he went to Santa Fe the first time?"

"I tried to, but I wasn't familiar with the territory, and I couldn't follow the trail in my mind," said Don.

Aubrey said, "That is the same thing that happened to me. I tried, but I just did not follow it. So, is that the way you want to go?"

"Yes, I think so. I have not completely made up my mind. That route sounded shorter and quicker. And you know me. I am always interested in shorter and quicker. The route is basically going from here north and west, until we can connect with the Red River. Then we will follow the Red until it fizzles out, several hundred miles west. As long as we keep going that direction, we will get to Santa Fe. I will see what I can find in the way of maps. I honestly do not think we can get lost. Using a map is always a good idea."

Troy said, "Albert, you and I should spend several days inventorying the merchandise in the store and shop. Then we can discuss what things I want to take to Albuquerque."

"That sounds good, Troy. Although, I am having a difficult time thinking about you not being a partner anymore."

"We are not going back to Albuquerque for a while, so we should have plenty of time to talk through everything. When the inventory is finished, at least you will know what you have. There will be plenty of time for us to work it out. I promise you that I will not leave until I get all your questions answered.

"OK, Troy, I will try to stop getting so anxious."

"We should go to the store and get started. I have no idea whether this will take a long time or go quickly. We can work on it this afternoon and it will give us an idea of where we are on the inventory."

Back at the store, Troy and Albert found the most recent inventory and the inventory from just before Troy left for Santa Fe. They spent the rest of the afternoon going through the paperwork.

The two inventories were similar, so it appeared that all they would need to do is compare the most recent inventory to the physical goods in the store and shop. It should not take more than a day or two.

At the end of the afternoon, Albert said, "Troy, what do you think?"

"Albert, the paperwork seems to be in order. Now we can spend some time comparing the paperwork to the goods on hand. Then we can do some planning. I think it should just take a couple of days."

"That would be great, Troy. We should go see how your brothers are doing in the shop. Then we can go have some supper and go by the Doc's office to see Ralph."

Don and Aubrey were in the shop looking at the facility and talking to the employees who worked there. They had continued to work on the equipment they had orders for. It was not certain what they would do if Ralph was not able to return to the shop. Clearly, he was the key to the operation.

"Hey guys, how would you like a little supper?" Troy asked, as he and Albert walked into the shop.

"I think my stomach would appreciate that," Aubrey said.

"Yes, I could do that," Don said. "Are we going to see Ralph before or after?"

"After," Troy said.

Supper at the hotel was slow coming out of the kitchen, so the guys had plenty of time to talk and even make a few plans.

Troy said, "Albert and I found all the current inventory paperwork. We should be able to compare it to the physical inventory in the shop in a day or two. The current inventory is much like the inventory from just before we left for Santa Fe. I did notice some new items I was not familiar with. I guess the business keeps changing. Just because you know what customers need today, does not mean you will know what they need tomorrow."

"That certainly seems to be true in the shop," Aubrey said. "The workers there are keeping busy now with a large order, but seem to be concerned about what they will need to do after that order is completed until Ralph comes back."

"I am concerned about that also," said Albert. "Ralph had a list of standard things they always needed to make, like small garden tools and hand tools. We only need so many of those for the store. Ralph did a good job of working with people on their bigger farm needs like cultivators, planters, and plows. I am sure they could keep busy making some of those items. If Ralph is not able to come back, it will be difficult to continue that part of the operation.

"I have known Ralph most of my life. We have certainly been almost like brothers for most of our adult life. If Ralph is not able to come back to work, it will be like part of my heart is gone. To me, this store and shop is more like a friendship than a business."

All four men had tears in their eyes when Albert stopped talking.

After supper was finished, Troy said, "We should go to the Doc's office and see how Ralph is doing."

When the doctor saw the four of them come in, he smiled and said, "Ralph's color is better. He has not woken up; but he looks like he is still there, at least."

The four of them went into the room where Ralph was lying. He did look amazingly better because of his color. The pallid look of the day before made him look like he was already dead. Now he looked like all he needed to do was open his eyes like Don did last year on the trail and he would be alright.

Each of the guys took turns talking to Ralph just in case he could hear them. They all wished him well and told him they would see him tomorrow.

It was late, so they left and went home. The brothers were still staying in the hotel. They anticipated moving into Troy's house as soon as they could clean it up a bit. Troy had closed it up tight before they originally left for Santa Fe; but there was no keeping out that Louisiana fine clay dust.

Tomorrow after they finished working, they would go to the house and sweep and dust everything.

Troy had a feeling that their inventory tomorrow at the shop would not last long. Albert had kept the paperwork in good shape, so he anticipated the physical goods would be in shape also. After all, he had already done some looking around and could not see any problem.

The next morning rain was pouring down hard. It was a perfect day to do an inside inventory, so Albert and all three brothers worked together in the store. By supper time, the rain had stopped, and the inventory was complete.

The group met again at the hotel for supper and a review of the day.

Albert said, "I am really surprised that we got the inventory finished in one day. Thank goodness for the rain. That really helped. It kept us all in the store and kept customers away. Ralph had a separate inventory for the shop since most of what they manufactured wound up on the store's inventory, only equipment and materials were on the shop inventory."

Aubrey said, "I would be glad to go over that inventory tomorrow, if you two want me to."

Troy said, "Aubrey, that would be great."

Albert concurred, so Aubrey would work on that inventory tomorrow. They decided that the paperwork was in the store. The shop had a tiny office. It was not a good place to store important paperwork.

The hotel had an especially good supper, so more time was spent eating than talking. After supper they took their nightly visit to the doctor's office.

Doc was in another good mood when the guys went in this evening. He said, "Ralph was looking better again today. I almost thought he moved a little this afternoon. Tomorrow should be an interesting day. Oh, but let me warn you that this time is likely to be dangerous. I have heard of times when a person was in a coma, began to look better for several days, and then died. I do not know what would cause that; but it could be their body going through shock. So, we will hope and pray that whatever causes that situation will stay away from Ralph."

They ended their day on a worrisome note, but a good one also. Ralph was still looking better.

Morning brought another heavy rain, so the Rampy brothers and Albert spent their morning in the shop and completed the inventory quickly. Most of the inventory was full of manufacturing equipment, the largest of which was a blacksmith forge. They kept this equipment busy most days bending and shaping metal and attaching metal pieces to create farming equipment.

Aubrey said, "Back home in Alabama, I did some part time work for a local blacksmith. I loved working on the forge; but usually I had to do other things. The blacksmith loved it too, of course."

"Ralph had been thinking about getting a new forge for the shop," said Albert. "He thought we could keep a second forge busy most of the time. I am not sure. He may have already ordered it. If Ralph is not here to run it, we will have to find another blacksmith. Ralph could do it all here in the shop."

"Albert, how have your sales of farm equipment gone this past year?" asked Troy.

"We have sold everything that Ralph and his crew have made. They have made more plows than anything else. Then after that would come cultivation equipment. Most of that was made to customer specifications. Planters worked well. We have not made as many of those as we would have liked. I think it will eventually be a big part of our farm equipment business. Farmers seem to trust themselves planting by hand more than doing it with a machine. But I think their thoughts about that are changing slowly."

"That is very interesting Albert," Troy said. "Most people do seem to be slow to change away from something they know and try something they do not know. I can understand that. I never was one to jump to something new when it was replacing something I already knew how to use. It is exciting to see how much is being sold out of the shop. That was the smallest piece of the business at first, and maybe it always will be. It is certainly growing."

Weather cleared just before noon and the inventory was done, so the four men went to the hotel again for lunch. They talked for two hours and then left the restaurant. Albert went to the store and the three brothers went to Troy's house.

Troy had closed his house up as tight as he could before he left a year ago to Santa Fe. Regardless, it was still filled with dust and mouse droppings. At least nothing seemed to be living in the house; well, except for the mice. He had asked a friend to come by the house earlier in the week to wash the bedding, so that was in good shape.

Other than the dust and mice droppings, the house was in good shape. It was a well-built house with large rooms and high ceilings. He wished that he could have one just like it in Albuquerque; but he would have to build it once he got back.

There was already a friend in Albuquerque building him a building he would use as a store; but he would wait until he got there to build a home. Where he would build it and what size it would be, were still questions for later.

Troy and his brothers did their best to sweep every room and wipe every shelf before the afternoon was over. The house was ready for them to move in. They would stay in the hotel one more night and move into the house tomorrow.

They met Albert again at the end of the day and went to the Doc's office. Ralph was looking better, and Doc was feeling positive. They all took turns talking to Ralph and telling him they were looking forward to him waking up.

When they left Doc's, Albert went home and the brothers sat on the front porch of the hotel and talked. They talked about all that had been done since getting to town and how things were progressing.

Aubrey raised the question. "Troy, are you planning to have a shop in Albuquerque like you do here?"

Troy thought about the question and said, "Aubrey, I do not know. Maybe someday, but not at first. I do not see the need for that now. The farms and ranches in that area seem to have different types of operations. They are more based on sheep and cattle than crops. Once we have been there a while, it may become clear that there is equipment they locals need. Would you like to run that sort of operation?"

"I think so, Troy. It has been fascinating to work in the shop, since we have been here. I think about it a lot."

"Well, Aubrey, once we get things rolling in Albuquerque, we can look for things that might be needed in the local area and that you could manufacture."

Don said, "Troy, have you thought about what you want to take back with us to Albuquerque? Do you have any idea how many wagons will be needed?"

Chuckling, Troy said, "It seems like there are only two things I have been thinking about lately. One is getting back to Albuquerque to see Justine and the other is what merchandise should we take back. So, yes, I have been making a list. I am trying to keep it short, but it keeps growing. I need to start thinking about how many wagons it would fill, but I have not done that yet.

"Don, would you check around town for wagons to see what is available? And while you are doing that, you might make some inquiries about the possibility of hiring drivers."

"I would be glad to do that. How long do you anticipate the trail home will be?"

"My guess would be six weeks. I hope it will not be much longer than that."

Don spent the next two days checking around town for wagons and drivers. He found that the market for wagons was good, but the quality of wagons was relatively poor. Men willing to drive wagons were plentiful; but drivers willing to go on a long caravan were not so common.

Finally on the third day, he found a business that made wagons that would work for them. The Petre brothers, Hans and Olaf, had been building cargo wagons for five years. Before that, they had built smaller wagons for local merchants who needed less capacity.

The Petres had eight wagons they were anxious to sell. A commercial hauler had ordered them, but was unable to pay for them when the wagons were finished.

Don told them that he and Troy would be back the next day to talk to them about the wagons.

13 | TRAIL TO HOME

That evening after supper, Albert and the Rampys went by the doctor's office to see Ralph.

Albert said, "Doc, did Ralph have a good day today?"

"There has not been any change that I have seen in the past three days. His heartbeat is stronger than it was and his color looks good. But, Albert, I am still concerned that he will not wake up. And, if he does wake up, I doubt he will be the same man as before. All we can do is pray and wait."

All the men spoke to Ralph as they passed by him on the way out of the office. They wished him well and told him they were praying for him.

Troy and Don went to see the Petre brothers the next morning.

The brothers were busy cleaning their shop when Don and Troy came in.

Don said, "Olaf and Hans, this is my brother, Troy. I brought him to talk about your wagons."

Hans came forward and shook Troy's hand vigorously while saying, "Hello, Troy. It is nice to meet you. I am Hans and this is my brother, Olaf. Don was telling us yesterday that you may be needing some cargo wagons. We have eight large cargo wagons that we would like to show you. That is more inventory than we usually have on hand, so we are certainly willing to deal with you on them."

Then he laughed and said, "Well, we do not want to give them away; but I think we can arrive at a reasonable price. Shall we go look at them?"

Two of the wagons were still in the shop and the other six were out back where they had been chained together.

Hans said, "Troy, all eight wagons are identical. We made them to carry a full load of rather heavy items, so I hope that is what you need. Their suspension was built as heavy as we know how to build it. As you can see, the suspension is made with different lengths of heavy metal leaves held together by metal brackets. Each wagon is made with strong wooden sides and back. They are bolted together with strong metal bolts. Each side or the back can be undone to allow easier access for cargo."

Olaf said, "Troy, is this the type of wagon you were looking for?"

"Yes, this is exactly the kind of wagon we are looking for. I would like all eight, if we can work out a good price."

Hans said, "We can go inside and talk about that over a cup of coffee."

The four men went inside the shop to discuss the wagons. They were startled to see Albert and Aubrey rush into the shop.

Albert said, "I just got a message from the Doc for all of us to come see him as soon as possible."

Troy and Don excused themselves and told Hans and Olaf they would be back later to finish talking about the wagons.

At Doc's office the news was not good. Doc met them at the door with tears in his eyes. He said, "Ralph has passed.

"This morning, he was looking the same as the past few days. Then about mid-morning, he seemed different somehow. I checked his pulse, and he did not have one. I tried to revive him, but could not get a pulse, no matter what I did. I have called for the undertaker to get a coffin ready. If you all want to see him before the undertaker comes, I will have him wait until you are finished."

They all went in and said their goodbyes to Ralph.

After their goodbyes, the body was taken to the mortuary. It was decided they would have a short memorial service at the cemetery in the morning.

Troy and Albert decided the four of them would have supper together at the hotel for their own short memorial.

It was especially difficult for Albert. He and Ralph had been friends most of their lives. He said, "I was still not prepared for this. Ralph and I have been friends for so long. I could not imagine he would die. Deep inside, I felt like he would recover and be the same person he always was. It will be difficult to go on without him. He and I grew up in the same area, but we did not know each other till our late teens. We were similar in age and our families knew each other. I thought at one time, he would marry my sister. But she decided to marry someone else. That is about the time we got to know each other and started traveling together.

"I just cannot believe it. I guess I had better get the word out to his friends about the memorial service in the morning. Aubrey, could you do me a favor? Would you go close the shop and store for the rest of the day. Tell everybody what happened and tell them about the service in the morning. We will open again tomorrow afternoon. I will spread the word to everybody else."

"I would be glad to, Albert. I will see you later."

Don and Troy left and went over to finish their dealing with Hans and Olaf.

Hans saw them arrive and invited them into the shop. He said, "Olaf and I heard about Ralph. We were sorry to hear it. We were good friends with him. A lot of our supplies and materials were ordered through his shop."

Troy said, "There will be a memorial service in the morning at the cemetery, if you can be there."

Hans said, "We will definitely be there."

Troy said, "It is sad. Ralph was my friend for only a few years, but he was special to me. Albert is going to have a hard time dealing with his passing. They had known each other for most of their lives.

"Well, I hate to talk business at a time like this, but I do need those wagons. What kind of a price were you thinking for them? What was the original price you were asking?"

Hans told him the original contract price for the wagons and Troy said, "Hans, that sounds like a fair price. I will take all eight of them at that price."

"Troy, we were thinking we could do a little better than that."

"Hans, I appreciate that, but let me pay the original price and I will be happy."

"Troy, that is extremely generous. Thank you very much. Just let me know when you need them, and I will have them ready."

"Hans, one more thing. Don said you might know some good drivers we might hire for a caravan out to Albuquerque?"

"Yes, I know enough good drivers to get you there. I will start talking to them. Please let me know when your start date will be as soon as you decide."

"I will, Hans. Don or I will be back in touch with you soon. It has been nice dealing with you."

"Troy, it has been a real pleasure dealing with you."

Supper with Albert and the Rampys started sad, but ended happily. It was more an Irish wake than a memorial. Albert reminisced about their younger days when it was a happier time. He also talked about their work in the store for the past few years. It had been a special time for them and their relationship. They had both made many new friends in New Orleans.

After supper, Don and Aubrey went to Troy's house, while

Troy and Albert went back to the store to finish talking about the coming changes.

After days of looking over the inventory, Troy had made a list of the items he wanted to take to Albuquerque as his portion of the store's value.

At the store, Troy said, "Albert, I gave you the list of items I have been thinking about taking; but that was dividing the store into thirds. Now that Ralph is no longer with us, what are your ideas about how to divide the business?"

Albert smiled and said, "Troy, that is a good question. But I do have an answer, I think. We have not really considered the buildings. The store building and shop are both yours, so I should start paying you rent."

"Albert, I know you have been concerned about running the store and the shop together. What are you thinking now about that? Do you think you can make it work?"

Albert smiled and said, "Troy, I think I have found a solution. I saw that your brother Aubrey enjoyed working in the shop. That gave me an idea. I asked him today if he would be willing to stay in New Orleans and run the shop. He said he would, if it did not put you and Don in too much of a bind going back to Albuquerque.

"I figured, since you have not sold your house, he could live there and run the shop for a salary paid by both of us out of Ralph's share of the business. Then eventually, we could make him a partner and give him Ralph's share. Of course, that would mean that you and I would still be partners in the shop for the time being. What would you think of that? Is it workable in your mind and can you do without Aubrey?"

"Don and I will really miss Aubrey, but I like your suggestion. We can discuss it with Aubrey and if he can live with it, so can I.

"By the way, I have made an agreement to purchase eight large cargo trailers to take the merchandise to Albuquerque.

When can we start loading that? And is there anything on the list that you do not have duplicates of and cannot stand to lose at this time?"

"I think we have duplicates of everything on your list in our inventory, so we should be fine. We could start loading as soon as you have the wagons, or we could wait until you have done everything you still want to do in New Orleans."

"OK, Albert, I think we should wait until a week from today to start loading. That should give me time to do a few more things and make sure we have plenty of drivers."

The next morning, the memorial had a good group of people. Numerous people shared their memories of Ralph, as they knew him. Then the coffin was lowered into the ground and a little dirt was shoveled on top. The group dispersed and the undertaker finished with his work.

It was a sad occasion, but happy at the same time. So many nice things were said about Ralph that it was an uplifting morning.

After lunch, Albert and Troy sat down with Aubrey to discuss his possible role in the store and shop. They discussed a salary for him as the shop manager and the likelihood of making him a partner in the operation in the not-too-distant future.

Aubrey was excited about running the shop and being part of the operation. He also liked the idea of living in New Orleans. The city and it's warm and hospitable citizens always appealed to him.

Of course, after Troy told Don about the new changes in New Orleans, he promised Don that he would also have a good job in his Albuquerque operation, if he would stay with him until then.

Don told him that he had no intention of staying in New Orleans, for which Troy was grateful. Replacing both brothers would have been almost impossible. He felt comfortable having at least one of his brothers with him on this long journey.

After that day, things started moving fast. Don notified the

Petre brothers that they would like the wagons the next week.

Then he started hiring drivers that could be ready the next week. One driver that the Petre brothers thought especially highly of was hired as a driver and driver foreman.

Don hired eighteen drivers, including the foreman, a cook, a cook's helper that had some medical training, and a mechanic.

When the caravan moved out, everyone would be wearing a pistol and carrying a rifle with their gear. The route they intended to take would be more direct than Troy and his brothers had taken previously. They would not go to St. Louis for supplies this time. Everything needed would be taken from Troy's store. There would be no need to take the route that was becoming known as the Santa Fe Trail.

The caravan would be taking essentially the same route taken by Bill Rampy when he first went to Santa Fe on his search to find new customers for Troy's New Orleans store. Of course, the route would not be going to Santa Fe, so they would turn toward Albuquerque at some point along their trail.

Bill Rampy's search for new business had been successful in finding new business for Troy's store and for finding Bill a wife, Frances.

Buying mules proved to be more difficult. Horses were more commonly used in the New Orleans area at the time for pulling wagons. Don was able to get five full teams of mules; but, to fill out their needs, he got three teams of draft horses.

The Caravan start date was decided to be the middle of the next week. Between now and then the wagons would be loaded, the drivers would get familiar with their animals, and the cook and helper would start working on meal preparation for the route. All the supplies needed would be purchased and a small wagon would be obtained for them to use as both a supply and cooking wagon.

Toward the end of the week, the three brothers and Albert set down to talk about the ongoing preparations.

Troy said, "Well, gentlemen, it is beginning to look like Don and I will be going to Albuquerque soon. What can you tell me about that?"

Don laughed and said, "Yes, we are going to Albuquerque. I am happy to say that five wagons are nearly ready to go. They are being kept in the shop until we go. The Petre brothers brought us a half wagon load of spare parts, which should really come in handy. Most of the drivers we have hired are working with their horses or mules. They should be in good shape and ready to go, whenever we have the wagons loaded. The cook and his assistant have all the food they need and are ready to go."

Troy said, "That is great, Don. I am half tempted to start early, but we will not. We have told the new drivers we will start mid-week and I want to stay with that."

"I agree, Troy. We do not want to tell them one thing and start changing it. The middle of this coming week will give us plenty of time to get the work done and not feel like we are having to scramble. Do you have all the information for the route we are going to take?"

"Yes, when Bill came back from Santa Fe, he gave me a detailed map of the route he took. He said the route should be good enough for wagons with a heavy load. It is an easy route to follow and there are several significant landmarks that should keep us on course.

"Exactly where we need to change our route to head more directly to Albuquerque instead of Santa Fe, is still a little unclear; but we can figure that out once we get in the area. I guess the worst thing that could happen would be to wind up in Santa Fe and need to go to Albuquerque from there.

"Once we make our route change it should not be long until we see a landmark that should confirm we are on the right path. There is a large individual mountain called Tucumcari Mountain. When we see that, we will know we are headed correctly. I am excited about taking Bill's old route. I enjoyed our route when we left St. Louis; but I am really looking forward to the new route."

Don said, "As I recall, Bill said he had some trouble with Indians on that original route. Do you think we should anticipate trouble with them as well? I think we should be prepared in case of trouble; but I am not going to worry about it too much. I have a feeling that as-long-as we leave them alone, they should leave us alone. Of course, I could be a fool; but that is going to be my attitude as we start the trip. I will see if it changes along the way. Bill told me that he thought he only had trouble because he was by himself and not traveling as part of a group."

Albert said, "I told all the employees in the shop and store that Aubrey will be running the shop. They are obviously sad about Ralph's passing, but are excited to have Aubrey running the shop. I imagine the men in the shop were afraid we might close the shop and they would lose their jobs. Aubrey and I told them about some of the new plans we have for the shop and that we might want to hire some additional people. I know that they felt good about that and more secure in their jobs. Troy and I have been keeping an eye on the load-out of the wagons and that is continuing to go well. It appears that it should be complete by Monday, so you can plan to leave on Wednesday."

Troy said, "Yes, everything seems to be going perfectly, so far. When the wagons are loaded, we can let the drivers and other workers take a couple of days off to spend with their families. Then we will gather back here on Wednesday morning at first light."

Troy was getting more and more excited that the return trip was getting so close. His thoughts about Justine and returning to her were getting stronger and stronger. On their trip to New Orleans, his mind was kept busy with the trip and what he needed to do once he got there. But now that the return trip was getting close, all he could think of was Justine and returning to the life he wanted to make for them in Albuquerque. It was hard to keep his mind focused on anything else.

The word was spread that as soon as the loadout was finished, everyone could have off until Wednesday morning. Operations, of course, continued at the store and shop, so Aubrey was busy. But Don and Troy spent time in town speaking to friends and telling them about the move to Albuquerque.

Troy had many business acquaintances to talk to. There were numerous storekeepers, three bankers, two lawyers, three preachers, four builders, two blacksmiths and a host of others. He wished them all well and told them he hoped they could keep in contact once mail service reached into his new area.

The weather had been good in recent weeks and promised to get better. Although, as everyone knew, it could change in a heartbeat. Troy and Don had been discussing the weather. Both had been thinking about problems that might arise and what they would need to do to get around them.

Biggest concern for travelers, particularly with wagons, centered around crossing rivers and muddy trails. Troy and Don had both studied their brother Bill's original route and the notes he made about it. They had a good idea of the areas of the most concern. They were looking at a long trip; but Troy was hoping it could be accomplished in six to eight weeks. The route appeared to be about twelve hundred miles, but could be much longer, if the conditions turned bad.

Finally, the wagons were loaded, tarped, and stowed away in the shop. The horses and mules were being cared for in two local corrals. The drivers would check them Tuesday night to make sure they would be ready to leave first thing Wednesday morning.

14 | LEAVING NEW ORLEANS

Everything was set and ready to go Tuesday night, so the caravan rolled out Wednesday morning as planned. Many friends and family were there to say goodbye and watch everyone leave.

When the handshakes, kisses, and goodbyes were finished, the caravan rolled out toward Albuquerque. The Mississippi River on the west edge of New Orleans was huge and powerful. The caravan would take a ferry across the river.

The ferry was large enough to take two wagons and teams across the river at a time. It was slow going because the Mississippi was running high and fast due to recent heavy rains upstream. Most of a day was spent getting everyone and everything across the river, so they made camp for the night not too far from where they had begun.

With sunrise the next morning, they were off again. Traveling west to the Atchafalaya River took most of that day. Camp was made on the east side of the river. The ground was swampy in most places, so the travel had been carefully done. The caravan would follow along the Atchafalaya until they met the Red River.

Their intent was to travel along the southern side of the Red River, so they needed to cross the river at some time. The lead scout would keep an eye out for a decent crossing. It would need to be a broad flat place with a gravel bottom if one could be found.

Tracks along the river provided a good trail in most places, although there was a good deal of mud here and there. Most of the area they rode through was heavily forested with many swampy areas near the river.

Don and Troy were both riding as lead scouts along the Atchafalaya. Troy stopped the caravan for a lunch break in the early afternoon.

Troy and Don were sitting near each other eating thick bread they had brought from their favorite café. Troy said, "What do you think of our route, so far?"

"Well, I wish it was drier and more solid. But, if I read Bill's notes right, the route should get progressively drier as we go west. I guess the landscape can change a lot in over 1,000 miles."

"That is for sure," said Troy. "I am certainly curious to see how it does change. It was fascinating on our first trip to Santa Fe; but that was several hundred miles north of here and was drier to start with. We still saw a wide variety of game animals along the way, and I suppose we will here also. I wonder if we will see large herds of Bison on this route like we did then? They were fascinating too. But from what Bill and Juan told us, we sure do not want to get caught in front of a stampede like they did."

"It was certainly interesting that those huge animals lived on that short grass covering the prairie there. I would have thought they would need big grass and shrubs to graze on, instead of that low-growing fine grass."

Two days later the caravan got to drier ground and were thankful for the better footing. The variety of both large and small game animals was surprising. They had even seen six or seven brown bears and too many deer to count. The caravan had brought enough food to eat for the entire trip; but it appeared the cook would be able to supplement that with about any game he would like to use.

The next day, the caravan lost its first wheel. The road had gotten bumpy and one large bump caused a wheel to loosen and finally come off. It was not broken and just needed some manpower to put it on and tighten it well. Then the caravan was on its way again.

Troy and Don were riding as scouts again the next day and found an area that looked like a good crossing. It was a wide area that looked flat and bright. That gave it at least the appearance of gravel.

Troy tried it out and thought it would work well. He talked to the foreman of the drivers. He and three long-time drivers looked at the area and felt good about it.

They proceeded across, driving one after the other without any trouble until the last wagon. That wagon had gotten off to one side about five feet farther upstream than the wagon ahead of it. All at once, the wagon dropped into a hole. The wagon jolted to the left and looked like it might turn over; but thankfully, the wagon had enough momentum to pull it through the hole and onto more solid ground. What looked like a possible disaster was over in seconds and turned out better than anybody could have hoped.

Shortly after they had crossed the river, the caravan got to the Red River. It was good that they were able to cross the river when they did, before they reached the Red River.

What trail they found along the Red River was not as good as the trail along the larger river; but it served the purpose anyway. It was firm and relatively smooth. The trail and the river meandered along through thick woods. Game was still abundant, as it probably would be along the entire trip.

The second day on the trail along the Red River, the Caravan drove near the town of Alexandria. There was an area to camp, so they spent the night and investigated the town.

Alexandria was adjacent to a French trading post that apparently had been in the area for decades. It was a busy community with a surprising number of travelers. Most of the traffic seemed to be going north and south from Baton Rouge, a large town to the southeast.

The caravan spent one night at Alexandria and got back onto the trail the next day. Staying any longer did not seem like a good idea. Towns, especially busy towns, provided too many distractions that could cause problems. If they were going to get to Albuquerque on Troy's schedule, distractions needed to be avoided.

It was not long past Alexandria before distractions were not an option. As the caravan got into what was until recently Spanish Territory, there were no more towns to be found. Occasionally there was a residence where someone was trying to make a living as a trader, trapper, and farmer, but that was not common. Soon they would be into Indian territory where they did not expect trouble, but they might find it anyway.

Landscape had not changed much since they left Alexandria. The grass was still tall and trees were abundant. A bear had not been seen in days, but deer and elk were plentiful. It rained about every other day, not heavily, and the ground was not swampy or even muddy.

The trees were getting a little fewer and farther apart. Finding an area to circle our wagons at night for safety was easier. By the time they stopped for the night, the cook and his helper had usually gotten far enough ahead of the main caravan, that supper was already well started. That left the cook to select their camp for the night. Thankfully, he was good at it.

The foreman of the drivers was responsible for posting guards at night and making sure they rotated when they were supposed to. That always worked well. Everyone wanted to feel safe in camp and having a good guard system was the way to make sure it happened.

After supper, some of the drivers wrote in their journals, some talked to friends, and some sang. Troy and Don usually talked about the day's ride and the next day. They also planned for the new store in Albuquerque.

Troy said, "Don, I have been thinking about Bill's notes. I was reading them the other day, and from his description, I would say we are close to where he ran into a group of Indians. It was not too far into Indian territory, as I recall. I think we should keep an eye out for Indians during the day; but not get too excited if we see them. Bill came to believe, and convinced me, that most Indians are not looking for a fight. So, he also thought that if we leave them alone, they should generally leave us alone. That is going to be my plan until maybe some young bucks change my mind." He laughed. "No, seriously, I think we should try to treat them the way we want to be treated."

"Sounds reasonable to me, Troy. I would certainly rather have them as friends than have them as enemies. Sometimes you can run into a person or group that is just mean for some strange reason. They are few and far between, thank goodness. So, I think we should treat people the way we want to be treated."

"Exactly, Don. Exactly. Wasn't that what our Ma used to say?"

"Yes, I am pretty sure she got that out of the good book."

"Yes, I am sure that is correct."

"Troy, have you been missing Justine yet?"

"Yes, I miss her just about every minute of every day. I cannot wait to see her."

Don laughed and said, "Oh, I know you miss her. I was only kidding. But I know something that you do not know."

"What is it that you know that I don't know?"

"Did you know that you talk in your sleep? And did you know that most of that talking is to Justine about something or the other? Or just calling out her name?"

"Are you kidding me? I don't really do that, do I?"

"Brother, you most certainly do. We really need to get you home soon, before you drive me crazy."

"Wow, I had no idea that I talked in my sleep. I apologize. I will try to stop doing that."

Don laughed and said, "Troy, I cannot imagine you will be able to do that. In fact, if you can do that, I will give you one hundred dollars as a wedding present."

"I will take it. Thanks, Don."

"But you have to stop it first."

"Well, I will try to stop, for your sake. But, frankly, the idea of calling out her name sounds pretty good to me, even if it is only in my sleep."

Don laughed and said, "OK. Well, we will just have to see what happens."

"Don, we should get some sleep. We can work on all this again tomorrow. And I will try to stop talking in my sleep."

The next morning, as had become the caravan's custom, everyone was up at first light getting their animals and wagons ready to go for the day. The cook already had breakfast cooking and coffee brewing.

Once everyone had finished breakfast and their morning ration of coffee, they were on the trail. Obviously, this trail was not commonly used because it was rough and not well-marked. The ground here was soft enough to make it easy to drive over. The area along the river was getting hilly, so the caravan stuck closely to the river as it wound its way through the hills. It appeared this might be the situation for a long time across this territory.

One good thing about sticking close to the river is that they would always be close to water. But the bad thing would be that they would also be close to those who came to use the river.

They could not avoid Indians forever, so eventually Troy and Don would have to test their theory about Indians.

That evening, it started to rain hard. They had already gotten circled up for the night under some large oak trees, so at least they had some protection.

By morning, the caravan could see that they had another problem, rising water. The water flowing out of the hills to the north was filling up the river to capacity and it looked like the trail was going to start flooding.

The cook had gotten up earlier than normal to prepare the breakfast and coffee. Drivers rushed through their breakfast and got ready to move out.

A scout had gone out at first light to look for a route that would move the caravan away from highwater. A good route was found, but it would mean the caravan would have to climb away from the river. Hopefully, the wagons would be able to move back nearer the river by the evening.

The higher ground was unfortunately not easy to follow. There was no ridge to stay on. Drivers had to go up and down a lot because of the valleys in between.

By the end of the afternoon, the wagons were finally able to go back to the trail by the river. All was well again. They found a large clearing in which to circle up for the night, so they stopped about an hour and a half earlier than normal.

It had been a hard day. The drivers struggled to make their desired distance; but, even with the difficulties of the revised route, the caravan had done well.

After a good supper of meat and vegetables, everyone got their evening chores completed and turned in for the night. They needed all the rest they could get.

Breakfast the next morning was about the same time as usual. Everyone was tempted to sleep in a bit; but they were feeling refreshed after the early evening, so they got up at first light.

Troy and Don had coffee together as usual. "Don, I think we are getting close to where Bill's notes first mention spotting an Indian village on his route. So, I suppose we should not be shocked if we see a village or group of some kind. When we do, I still think we should try to avoid them, if we can."

"But if we cannot avoid them," Don said, "we are still thinking that we will just act as friendly as we can and proceed past them?"

"Yes, that is what I think we should do. That worked well on our way to Santa Fe. I know this is a different group of people here; but, I suspect we will all think the same way. Hopefully, whatever happens will not happen quickly and startle us."

It was a beautiful day, and it appeared the caravan would make good progress. The trail was solid and smooth, so both horses and mules could make good time. For whatever reason, some road conditions favored some animals over others. The difference was not usually large; but some days it was surprising.

By the lunch break, the drivers felt good about the distance they had traveled.

After a short break, the caravan was starting up again when an Indian hunting party was noticed about three-quarters of a mile ahead. There were probably only ten or twelve braves. The distance was too great to decide what tribe they might belong to. Bill's notes indicated he had seen Wichita Indians in this area on his journey. The braves had crossed the river and were heading south up one of the valleys that flowed down to the river.

The hunting party appeared to be on the track of a small herd of deer that had been seen earlier as the caravan was stopping for their break.

Troy and Don were out front of the caravan as scouts. They were riding close together to talk.

Don said, "I can imagine those braves catching up to those deer and flushing them back in our direction. Should we wait to see what happens?"

"No, I think we should go ahead. If we run into them, we will just wave as they run by. I do not think we will startle them much. They have probably seen us already. This will give us a chance to see if they are wanting to avoid us. Of course, if we do not see them, it does not prove they wanted to avoid us. They might be two miles up the valley by the time we get to the mouth of the valley anyway."

Fifteen minutes later as the caravan got to the mouth of the valley, Don's previous thoughts showed to be accurate.

Just in front of the caravan, the small herd of deer flashed in front of the caravan with the hunting party just behind.

The two groups were within three hundred feet of each other. The caravan stopped and the hunting party continued at a run.

Three braves raising their bows was the only acknowledgement between the two groups.

"That was interesting," Troy said. "I would not have assumed we would get that reaction." He laughed a nervous laugh. "We will have to see what happens next time."

"I am not anxious to see what happens next time," said Don. "But I am curious also."

The caravan continued to move west at its normal pace. Troy was obviously eager to get back to Albuquerque. Things were going well and he did not want to rush the caravan.

As the caravan rolled on, the trail got into an area where the ground was hard and rocky. The caravan slowed its pace to keep the wagons from bumping excessively on the rocky trail. It appeared the river, at that point, had cut across a naturally rocky area. The caravan did not care to move to the north side of the river at this point; but, if it had, this area probably would have given them the chance.

"Don, in Bill's notes he mentioned changing from the south side of the river to the north side and then back again several times. Thank goodness he was not driving a wagon. It would have been a hard thing to do."

"That is for sure. But he never would have taken a wagon anyway, unless he had taken a caravan like we did. He wanted to avoid any contact with Indians, just on the off chance they might be unfriendly. He must have had a fascinating trip. I wish I had been with him. Can you imagine how it felt to be by yourself in a new area, with people you didn't know and did not know how they would react to seeing you. The guy has guts. That is for sure."

"I agree with that. He does have guts.

"Speaking of Bill, I cannot wait to see him again. Once we get settled down in Albuquerque, we need to take a trip to Chihuahua."

"I agree. I would love nothing better than seeing Bill and Frances and her family. Oh, and speaking of family or family to be, have you been thinking of Justine much?" He laughed with a mischievous laugh.

"Don, I really cannot express to you how I have been thinking about Justine. Occasionally, and only occasionally, I can manage to think of something else. So, brother, if you mention Justine again, I may decide to knock you off your horse."

"Ok, Ok Troy. I get it. I will try to quit mentioning Justine. But all I wanted was to be able to tell her when we get back to Albuquerque that you would not quit talking about her."

"I see, Don. Not a bad idea. However, it really is sort of painful to be reminded of her. It makes me keep worrying about her. And while I am sure she is alright; it still makes me worry because I know that anything can happen."

"I will not mention her again. I did not know it was painful to you. But believe me brother, I know that Justine and her daughter must be doing well. I can feel it in my bones that she is ok and just waiting for your return."

"Thanks, Don. I appreciate your confidence. I feel she is ok also. I will be much better when we get there. We need to find a good spot for the night. The spot up in front of us looks like it might work. We should go look at it."

The caravan spent the night at the spot. It was near the water, but a little higher in case the water rose during the night. There was also plenty of tree cover in case of rain.

It was a good night. The sky was clear and there were millions of stars in the sky.

In the morning, breakfast was eaten quickly, and the caravan was moving forward by shortly after dawn. It was generally agreed that on the most beautiful days, the caravan should make as much time as possible. And this day promised to be one of the most beautiful days so far.

The trail was good also. Sandy soil along the way made for smooth riding, so the horses and mules could proceed at whatever pace they felt comfortable.

By their noon break, the drivers generally felt this had been their best morning yet. There had been no problems of any kind and they had maintained a good speed for the entire morning.

Something happened in late afternoon that had slowed them down. The caravan got to an area along the river that spread out for several miles. It was an area of marshland that looked like an excellent area for hunting ducks or geese.

The area reminded Troy and Don of an area on their first trip to Santa Fe where they had stopped for a duck hunt. Troy talked to the driver foreman and mentioned a duck hunt to him. He liked the idea and suggested they circle the wagons for the night, even though it was still early yet. Then he talked to all the drivers about a hunt.

All the men liked the idea and wanted to participate in the hunt. A strategy session was held, and the hunt proceeded.

While the hunt was underway, the cook and his assistant started preparing a fire for the ducks. They also prepared some carrots and potatoes for roasting and started cooking them.

The hunt went quickly and yielded twenty large ducks and three geese.

Everyone had a good time. Troy felt good that they all had the opportunity to relax for a while and that the cook had a chance to supplement their rations.

Supper was almost like a party atmosphere, with more than the normal amount of talk and joking. The talk lasted till late in the evening.

At breakfast there was still some duck and goose left that was quickly cleaned up and washed down with extra coffee. Then the caravan was back on the trail. Everyone was hoping that another opportunity like that might come along again before they got to Albuquerque.

It was a beautiful morning and by lunch break, the wagons had made even more miles than normal. After a short lunch, they were anticipating another high mileage day when a vision to the west drew the wagon drivers up short.

A large Indian village was about a mile ahead of them. Thankfully, it was across the river, so the caravan did not have to plan how to go around it. But the sight of a different culture living along the hills above the river did cause them to stop and stare for a long time.

It was not clear what kind of Indians these were that lived in large domed houses. There seemed to be several hundred family members.

The caravan continued to the west on the south side of the river. As the wagons approached the Indian camp, some of the Indians seemed startled at first; but they finally settled down and went about their business.

There was a great deal of activity. Women appeared to be working on large hides, while men seemed to be either helping with the hides or working on weapons. The children were spread out playing what appeared to be a variety of games.

When the two groups were directly across the river from each other, both groups were looking at each other with an unusual intensity. Some of each group raised their hands in a wave or salute.

As the caravan continued past the camp, both groups continued staring at each other until finally they quit when they could barely see each other anymore.

The conversation over supper that evening was full of talk about the Indians. The drivers had all seen Indians before in Louisiana, but nobody had seen them in large groups like today.

Even Troy and Don, who had seen lots of Indians, thought this was an unusual day.

Don said, "I wish I knew what group of Indians that was. I have no Idea. Bill's notes mention several types of Indians, but not with enough detail for me to tell them apart. If I had to guess, I would say they were Osage."

"Yes, I would guess that Osage is correct; but I am not sure. Did you see those large hides they were working on? I think we are getting close to bison territory. Their braves probably just got back from a hunt. It would be interesting to eat buffalo; but unless we could kill a small one, I would not want to do it. A big animal like them would be a world of trouble to kill, skin, gut and cook. If our cook would want to do that, I could understand. But I would not suggest it to him."

Don was laughing to himself and said, "I agree. I would not want to clean and cook one either. But I was just thinking a coat made from one of those hides would certainly be warm in the winter. It would look a bit unusual though; but it would be comfortable. People would think you were a real honest to goodness mountain man. That is not one of my ambitions in life."

Troy said, "Since I assume bison are close, we should keep an eye out for them. We do not want to stumble into a large herd and get them stirred up."

15 | THE CANYON

Keeping an eye out for bison was not necessary. In fact, the caravan did not have to find them at all. They found the caravan.

A day after the caravan passed the Indians, the group woke to a startling sight. They were literally surrounded by what appeared to be a thousand bison. There were bison on both sides of the river and both sides of the caravan.

When the cook was beginning preparations to start his fire for breakfast, there was just enough light to see what had happened during the night. The last thing he wanted to do was to startle the massive herd. He did not know what to do, so he talked to Troy and the driver foreman.

It was decided that everyone would be woken up and told of the herd surrounding them. They would all get up slowly and stay with their wagons. Once the bison moved far enough away, the animals would be hitched to the wagons and the caravan would slowly move out.

However, the assumption that the bison would play their part in this drama willingly did not go well. Two hours after the men got up and made ready to hitch their wagons, the bison had not moved.

The cook finally started a fire and made coffee. He passed around the coffee with some day-old biscuits and beef jerky.

By the time for the normal mid-day break, the bison had finally moved far enough away that everyone got their wagons ready to move.

It had been a morning like none other. Being inside a bison herd amazed everyone. Even the men who had been near bison before, had never been that close.

The bison were large powerful animals that seemed in some ways almost tame, although we knew they were not. The caravan, being in the middle of the herd, saw them up close and were surprised by their gentleness.

But nobody wanted to try to get friendly with them. That probably would not have gone well. They might look gentle but could turn defensive immediately. That is why the caravan worked all morning at not making them react.

When the caravan finally rolled out, the group knew they would never be in a situation like that again, so they relished the opportunity.

The caravan spent the rest of the afternoon and early evening on the trail. When they finally settled in for the night, the entire group must have wondered what would be with them at camp in the morning.

As one would expect, nothing was in camp with them the next morning or the morning after that, or any morning after that for the rest of the journey.

Troy and Don were going to ride lead scouts today. As they were getting ready, Troy said, "It just doesn't seem right to not wake up in the middle of a bison herd." Then he chuckled.

"I agree, Troy. There was something inspiring or maybe terrifying about waking up in the middle of a herd that big. At least we did not wake up in a huge pack of wolves. Now, that would have been terrifying."

"It will be interesting to see what the rest of this journey will bring. I would bet you that our next new surprise will involve animals of some sort."

"Troy, that is a pretty easy call, since all we ever see, besides the occasional Indian camp, is animals."

"But Don, what animal will be next is the big question."

"Well, we should move this caravan forward and just see what will be next."

Don and Troy were both laughing that afternoon when their question about 'what animal' was answered.

They were both riding together and dropped over the top of a hill along the river when they saw an expanse of elk that was surprising. What looked like two large herds of at least fifty bison each were spread out on both sides of the river.

The river was unusually wide at this point. It appeared the river flowed over a layer of smooth rock, making this spot a natural crossing for both animals and man. There was also a herd of deer on the south side of the river, not too far from the elk.

The cook, who was on the lookout for fresh meat, asked Troy if he could hunt for one or two small animals. He was given permission and took three people with him for the hunt.

Elk was eaten that evening and the next day at lunch. Venison was eaten for supper the next evening.

The fresh meat was a treat. And it was special, just to see the animals in the wild, in such large numbers. This country was so large and wide open, that the herds of animals were enormous also.

It was unclear how much longer the river would last. It had been getting shallow in recent days. Maybe that was because there had not been much rain yet. It might also be because they were getting closer to the source of the river.

Bill's notes on his trip through this area talked about the river getting shallow as he followed it west. He also mentioned that eventually the river would turn into a stream as it came through a magnificent canyon. On the far end of the canyon, the stream would reach its beginning. From that point on, the caravan would have to pick a route to Albuquerque, with no river to follow.

Bill was heading to Santa Fe, so he took a route to the northwest. The caravan will find a route a little more directly west.

Still being on the flat prairie, it appeared they were not near the canyon Bill mentioned as being so spectacular.

Troy had been carefully following the notes his brother kept on his journey west. Clearly, there were things in the notes that, if missed, could cause them to take a wrong turn. Troy felt good about the directions and thought he had followed them to the best of his ability. He felt confident they were on the correct route. It was just a matter of time.

However, it appeared they were miles from any spectacular valleys. All they could see in front of them was prairie, and it was short grass prairie at that. There was nothing to see that looked like the beginnings of canyons.

There had been hills and valleys at many places along the river, but the land had gotten more and more flat in the last few days. Oh, the land had its own beauty, so you had to admire that; but you could not deny how flat it was. Some places it seemed like you could see for miles. And that is the way it was at this point.

There had been herds of bison, elk, and deer over the past few days, but there was not much to see other than that.

Then gradually the land did start to change. Slowly it got a little rougher and hillier.

The water that had been a river was now a stream. Occasionally, other small streams fed into it. Those streams were apparently from run-off from rains or from natural springs.

When the caravan circled up that evening, Troy felt good about their progress and thought the canyon could not be far away.

Sitting by their campfire that evening, Don asked, "Troy, what are you thinking about our location? Are we getting close to the canyon that Bill mentioned several times in his notes?"

"Yes, I think we are. The land has acted just like Bill mentioned. He said it was flat for miles and then started to change. He said it would get rougher and then hilly. And then he said the land turned into a canyon around him. Well, it has been getting hillier for the past few days.

"I am getting the sense that we are almost to the area he was talking about. And he discussed that area in such detail, I am excited to see it. His description of the canyon walls, the color of the soil and rocks and the animals. I want to get there and see it through my eyes now that I have "seen it" through his notes. I think we will be sitting in that canyon tomorrow night and enjoying the scenery."

"I hope you are right, Troy. I am getting more and more excited to see the canyon also."

The next morning as the caravan started, most members of the caravan started with the intent to find the canyon and the picturesque scenery Troy had been promising for days. They knew the canyon would gradually appear along this series of short hills as the rapidly diminishing river wound its way west.

The trail was meager and the area was getting more beautiful. Troy found their journey down this one river amazing. First in Louisiana, the river flowed deep and wide through forested areas. Then as the river got out of Louisiana into Spanish territory, the river was still strong, but the land was less forested. The land was generally flat and there were hills here and there.

Gradually, over what Troy thought was five hundred miles or so, through Spanish territory, the river, and the land it wound through had many changes.

The land got drier and drier as they went west. Consequently, the river got smaller and drier.

Now, the river was still flowing, but it was more of a stream than a river. There was plenty of evidence that the stream was pointing the caravan toward the canyon, but there was no canyon yet.

The caravan rolled on until the early evening when the foreman and Troy picked a campsite. Tomorrow, the caravan would look again for the canyon. They had been through a great deal of beautiful country; but the canyon was still illusive.

The next morning, it did not take everyone long to get up, have breakfast, and start on the trail. Excitement ran through the group. It was not that they had never seen a canyon before. The excitement was because the canyon they were looking for was supposed to be especially unusual.

Scenery along the river was starting to get more dramatic as they rode along. The Caravan obviously had a way to go.

By mid-afternoon, Troy and Don felt like they were starting into part of the canyon. "Don, I think we are about to the lower reaches of the canyon. The hills are on both sides of us now. I will be surprised if we are not at the exciting part of the canyon by the time we reach camp tonight. Bill mentioned in his notes that once he got to what he felt was the start of the canyon, it really bloomed from then on for the next few hours. He expressed amazement at how fast it happened."

"I am certainly curious to see it. I hope we have not built it up too much in everyone's minds. I know it sounded especially dramatic in Bill's notes."

"Don, I do not think we will have too long to wait. Look there in the distance. I think we will have plenty to see soon."

The canyon walls were beginning to rise higher as they followed the small river west. In the distance were some rather serious looking storm clouds. What would happen to them if they were caught in this canyon with rising water was a big concern. Troy and Don were both beginning to think about the problems they could have.

Don said, "Those clouds in the distance scare me a little. If it becomes a gully-washer up ahead, what will we do with the wagons?"

"Hopefully, when we circle up for the night, we can pick a spot high enough above the river that we should not have a problem. If between now and then, it starts to look dangerous, we can camp early."

"Troy, one other thing Bill's notes mentioned about this canyon is that it is sort of like a box canyon. The walls of the canyon get bigger and bigger and then the canyon ends. He apparently did not have too much trouble getting his horse out of the canyon; but I wonder how difficult it will be to get our wagons out of the canyon?

"If we cannot get the loaded wagons pulled out of the canyon by our animals, that will be a problem. Maybe as we go farther and farther into the canyon, we should keep an eye out for escape routes, just in case we need one."

"That is an excellent idea, Don. I will mention that to the foremen and some of the drivers."

As the caravan rolled on toward the canyon, the hills on each side of the river got higher and farther apart. At first, they were a deep red. Then deep red striped with cream and pink.

By the time the caravan stopped for the night, the hills were probably three quarters of a mile apart and one hundred feet high.

Troy and the foreman had found an open spot thirty feet above the river. It provided adequate space and safety from any flash floods.

The cook got busy preparing the evening meal while the drivers tended the horses. Troy, Don, and the foreman rode ahead about two miles to scout the route for the next day.

Don said, "It looks like tomorrow will be a spectacular day."

"I agree," said Troy. "It should be beautiful."

The foreman, Armstrong, said, "I am less concerned about the beauty than I am about how we get out of this canyon at the river's end, if it is a boxed canyon."

Troy said, "I am confident we can find a way out. Even if we need to backtrack. Surely, we will find a place suitable to get the wagons out of the canyon. Each evening for the next couple of days, we can ride out on a scouting mission preparing for the canyon's end. When we find the canyon's end, then we can start our search for the best way out of the canyon. In the meantime, we can keep looking for possible escape routes."

That night the caravan slept under a beautiful sky full of stars, with only the occasional coyote calling its mate or friends. There was no rain, which all the drivers were happy for.

In the morning. Troy and the foreman decided it would be a good day to stop and make small repairs on the wagons and other equipment. The wagon axles were greased and the animals rested. The beauty of their campsite was the inspiration for the day's rest; but it had come at a good time.

The cook and his assistant had used the extra time to make large pans of peach cobbler, with dried peaches they had brought from New Orleans. They also tried to catch up on their bread making. Fresh bread had almost become a thing of the past, since the caravan had been moving so fast.

Cobbler and fresh bread with supper put everyone in an especially good mood. The evening was filled with conversation and even some singing. Coyotes in the distance joined in with the singing. Everyone had a feeling that tomorrow would be a great day.

The conversation started anew in the morning with coffee and fresh bread. It did not take the drivers long after a cup of good coffee to get to their rigs ready for the day. They all knew it would be an exciting day.

The canyon walls continued to rise as the caravan rolled west along the river, that was just a stream now. It was certainly beautiful and no longer what you would call a river.

During their scouting ride that afternoon, Troy and Don enjoyed the canyon as it blossomed before them.

Troy said, "I wish Bill was here to enjoy these sights with us. He certainly described it well in his notes. These canyons are unbelievable. Bill described them as being hundreds of feet high and almost looking like the skirt on a fancy Spanish dress. I can certainly see what he was saying. These canyon walls are so high, it does make me wonder how difficult it will be to get the wagons out at the west end. I just have a feeling that it will not be that difficult when we get there. I do not think backtracking will be in our future."

"I sure hope you are right, Troy. I have the same feeling. And, if Bill's notes are accurate, it will not be long before we get to the end of the canyon. Then we will know for certain."

There were dangerous looking clouds again in the west, so the caravan found a good spot well above the creek to stop for the night.

It was not long after supper when the storm broke. The sky was filled with lightning, wind, and rain. Everyone hunkered down in the wagons under the tarps to protect themselves, particularly from the lightning. Some of them had never seen lightning that strong and frequent. It was so close, that whenever a lightning bolt struck, the noise of the thunder sounded like being in the middle of a cannon barrage.

As quickly as the storm came, it was over. Then it was light again. The sun was just about to drop below the canyon wall on the west. The sight was incredible.

The water started to rise in the creek. It was not long until run-off from the canyon walls was filling the "creek" again, and it looked like the river they had considered it to be until recently.

Everyone was glad they set their camp on another high spot that evening.

Don said to Troy as they looked out over the growing water, "Well, there is the Prairie Dog Fork of the Red River. And I think we can call it a river again tonight. It is surely more river than stream. Maybe it got mad at us for calling it a stream and wanted to show us it was not finished yet."

"I hope it is done rising for tonight," said Troy. "If it keeps getting higher, it might still get up to the wagons."

"I think it has stopped rising," said Don. "So, we should be ok. I hope everything was tied down good and nothing got washed away. That was an amazing rain. I have seen one or two like that before, but that one was awesome."

By morning, the water was back down to its normal level. The only evidence of the storm was all the debris left behind in the shrubs and trees along the stream. It also left patches of mud here and there. Fortunately, most of the ground was sandy, so the wagons could get by without any problems.

The caravan moved out slowly, trying to avoid the worst areas of mud and standing water in holes in the riverbed. The view was even more spectacular than the day before because rain left the shrubs and trees wet, which brought out their colors more vividly. The walls of the canyon were also more colorful.

The canyon snaked around as it approached what appeared to be its end. This was the beginning of the canyon and the beginning of the river. Erosion had made the canyon several hundred feet deep at this point. Of course, there was no telling how large the watershed was that fed into the river.

Troy, Don and two more scouts had gone out as the canyon seemed to be coming to an end. Their intent was to find a path gentle enough that wagons could easily roll up out of the canyon. As rocky as this part of the canyon was, finding a smooth path out looked difficult.

The men took off to the west in two groups. Troy and Don went more directly west and would follow the canyon wall around. The other two would follow the stream to see where it entered the canyon.

By mid-afternoon, the two groups had run into each other. Neither group had found a path that would work, so they continued their search together.

The first thing they found was an unusual column-shaped rock formation. Like so many natural wonders in the canyon, they had to stop and wonder how this could have been created.

Passing by the formation, the group soon found a well-used trail leading toward the west canyon wall. When it looked like the trail was about to end, it turned sharply to the right and continued past an enormous boulder. From there, a twenty-foot-wide trail gradually made its way from the bottom of the canyon all the way to the western rim.

As the four scouts stopped at the top of the trail and gazed back down across the canyon, the view was awe inspiring.

Troy said, "It is incredible to imagine how any of this canyon was created. Only the hand of God could have done this. And isn't it nice that he created this trail for us to be able to get out of the canyon?"

Don laughed and said, "I think he may have made it for the Indians that live around here. It appears they are the ones who have been using it. With all the evidence we saw of them during our time in the canyon, I would say they must live in the canyon a large part of the year."

"You have me there, Don. I agree the Indians must be the ones who use this trail the most. I doubt there has ever been any other white men in this canyon. Oh, there have probably been Spaniards passing through, but not to live here. We have certainly not seen any evidence of them living here.

"We have found what we need. Now we should find the easiest way to the caravan."

Finding the caravan again was not difficult. The wagons had not gone far before Troy and the others got back to them.

Troy talked to the foreman about how the caravan needed to proceed in the morning. But, for now, they decided to set camp and spend one more night in the canyon.

Camp that night was fun for everyone. There was singing, playing instruments, and even a little dancing. The entire caravan knew this would be their last night in this interesting, entertaining, and enjoyable location. Tomorrow, they would be on their way to what would surely be much drier territory.

After a short night, the wagons with full water barrels moved out toward the cut where they would get out of the canyon. It was a hard pull and did not take long to get the caravan out of the canyon. From there, their trail would be more-or-less directly west to Albuquerque.

16 | TRAIL TO HOME

The land at the top of the canyon was amazingly flat. In fact, it was so flat that there was no other topic of conversation until the mid-day break. By then the land had begun to roll a little and they had seen a dry creek.

Everyone knew the land between where they currently were, and Albuquerque would all be dry. There may be the occasional creek, but most would be dry. That is why they had taken the time in the canyon to refill their water barrels for their animals and themselves.

Don and Troy were riding as scouts again because they had gotten into that habit. It would have been difficult for either of them to drive a wagon. But that was ok because their drivers had done well. Aside from a few minor illnesses or injuries, everyone had been well for the entire trip.

Don chuckled and said, "Troy, are you still thinking of Justine every minute of every day? Or have you been able to put her out of your mind long enough to think of something else?"

"I have been able to think of a few items of business for once we get back. But, yes, it is mainly Justine. However, I think less about how much I love her and more about her and her daughter's safety. Albuquerque is a nice town, but there is a rough element that comes through town from time to time."

Don said, "I would certainly agree with that, especially considering your last incident in her store. But she did well in that. And she will probably do well if there is ever another incident."

"Yes, I certainly agree with that. Just knowing it happened one time concerns me. I pray for them a lot and know their family does too. I still cannot wait to get there."

Don said, "I cannot wait to get there either. And I do not even have a girlfriend waiting for me. I am just anxious to get somewhere I can call home and settle down."

"That will be nice, Don. And you know what? I bet it will not take long for you to find a girlfriend once we get there. With all your innate Rampy charm, surely there will be a beautiful girl that will not be able to resist you for long."

"Thanks, Troy. I know you are making fun of me, but I will accept it as a compliment and hope there is some magic in it. How many days do you think it will take us to get home?"

"I am thinking it should take eight days. I hope that is correct; but, not having been across this land, I do not know for sure. If we are on the right path, we should be seeing a good landmark in a few days. Mount Tucumcari is on one of Bill's maps that someone had given him before his trip to Santa Fe. When we see the mountain, it will confirm we are on the correct path and give us some idea of how far we must go."

The first day out of the canyon went well. There was no definite trail and the ground was smooth and not rocky.

The caravan was able to move at a good pace. They had to cross several streams. There was little water in them and the bottoms were solid.

Caravan speed was usually about four to five miles per hour. Time to cross streams and make repairs was extra. Considering all this, Troy was still hoping they would make forty to fifty miles per day.

The caravan stopped briefly once in the mid-afternoon under a grove of trees. They had been moving well and did not want to lose any momentum that they had going.

By evening, they felt they had done almost fifty miles. Their intent was to get up early in the morning, have a quick breakfast, and get back on the trail.

It had been a good day considering the miles traveled. And it had been easy because of the flat, smooth ground. The drivers were still intending to get into their bedrolls a little early, to rest up for tomorrow.

Don and Troy sat around a small campfire talking about the day.

Troy said, "It was a good day today. I would love every day to be like this one."

Don said, "For a day when we had no defined trail, this day was awesome. I wonder if we will get on an established trail at some point or if we will continue to make our own way?"

"I am hoping we eventually run into a path of some kind; but, if every day is like today, it will not make much difference."

"Yeah, Troy, I agree with that. It was surprising to cover so much territory when we had no trail to guide us. Certainly, by the time we get to Mount Tucumcari, there will be a trail from there to Albuquerque. With the mountain being a landmark, lots of travelers have gone by there. And most of them would be going to or coming from Albuquerque."

Troy said, "By the time we get to the mountain, we might start seeing other travelers. It has been a long time since we saw anybody. On the route we have been taking, the only travelers were Indians in a few places. Hopefully, we will get to the mountain in two days. That will be exciting. It will indicate not only that we are on the right path; but also, that we are getting close to home. And I am getting close to Justine."

After a quick breakfast, the caravan was on the trail toward Mount Tucumcari, or at least hoped they were heading that way.

There was still no trail. The conditions were the same, so they should make good time.

Hopefully, they would be near Mount Tucumcari either tonight or tomorrow. The drivers would need to keep a good lookout for the mountain both to the north and south in case they were off course.

There was no sign of the mountain by the time they camped for the night, so everybody was excited about tomorrow.

Armstrong, the foreman, stopped by to see Don and Troy after supper. He said, "How are you guys doing? I have a feeling it will not be long before we get you home to Albuquerque. Are you getting excited?"

"Yes, we are getting more excited than you can imagine," said Troy. "There is a lady there who I think is special and I cannot wait to see her."

"What does she do there, Troy?"

"She runs a store. It is a store for women's dresses, shoes, and other items."

"Well, Troy, I hope we get there soon. That mountain should be coming up on the horizon tomorrow. And then it is only a few more days until you get home.

"Then the guys and I will have to head back to New Orleans. Of course, that should not take too long with us all riding horses. We should do it in half the time without the wagons. That should be nice."

Troy said, "Yes, I hope it will be.

"Armstrong, I appreciate your work a great deal. It has been nice to have someone with your experience running the caravan. If you are ever back in Albuquerque and are looking for a job, just let me know."

"I certainly will, Troy. Thank you very much.

"Now, I had better get to sleep. We are going to hit it hard in the morning and go find that mountain."

The camp was buzzing with activity by daybreak. It seemed that everyone was as excited as Troy and Don to be reaching the destination of the trip. After all, it was human nature to want to reach a conclusion. After all these weeks the caravan was almost to an end.

Of course, the drivers still had to go home once the trip was over; but that would not be hard compared to the trip to Albuquerque.

Late in the afternoon one of the scouts reported he could see Mount Tucumcari off to the north several miles. Troy and Armstrong agreed that it was the mountain.

The caravan had missed the mountain, but was not too surprised. At least they were close enough to have it for a landmark and that was the point. The route was adjusted to the north enough to get them on a more direct path for Albuquerque. They felt better about their route now.

The caravan drove another two hours before stopping for the night.

Camp that night was even more excited than the night before. And the scouts had found a trail they would be using tomorrow.

This was only the second night since the canyon that camp would be made in a grouping of trees. The route had been mainly across prairie, but was now in a forested area.

As the sun was coming up the next morning, Troy and Don sat down with many of the drivers to have breakfast and coffee. This had been their normal habit since the start of the caravan. They liked to talk to the drivers, especially about the wagons and animals. If there was a problem with either, it was vital to get it fixed quickly.

At this point in the caravan, everything was going smoothly. There had been a few minor problems with the several wagons initially; but the repairs went well and were still lasting. The mules and horses were good stock and had had few problems.

There was no doubt that the wagons and animals would last the next few days to Albuquerque.

Troy was happy that the drivers were excited to be getting to Albuquerque, so they could turn around and go home to New Orleans.

The morning went well, so they took a longer than usual break for lunch. It appeared they would be getting to the Pecos River before they stopped for the night.

Don and Troy were riding scout and were both somewhat familiar with this territory. It was obvious the Pecos River was near; but they were not familiar with the crossing. Once they got to the river, there might be a need to look around for the best spot to cross.

In the past two days, Troy had seen several travelers coming from the direction of Albuquerque; but he had not talked to them about the best crossing on the Pecos. Now, he wished he had.

Troy let Armstrong know he and Don were going to ride ahead to see if they could find the best crossing. By the time the caravan got to the river, hopefully Don and Troy would have found the crossing.

When the Rampys got to the river, finding the best crossing was not difficult. They just looked for an area along the river that had the most tracks into the water. One spot near where they got to the river easily stood out as the most popular spot.

They both tried it out and had no problems. The water was deeper than they thought it would be. They did not think the wagons would have any problems.

A traveler was approaching the river from the Albuquerque side, so they stopped and talked to him.

Troy said, "Hi, I am Troy Rampy, and this is my brother Don. We are riding as scouts for a caravan headed to Albuquerque. I assume that is where you are coming from?"

"Yes, I came through there; but I am not from there. My name is Isaac Gonzales. My family lives about seventy-five miles southwest of Albuquerque."

"Isaac, we are intending to make Albuquerque our home. I am going to open a dry goods store there. There is a caravan following us with our first inventory. So, the next time you are in Albuquerque, please stop by to see us."

"I will, Troy. Hey, you might have less competition after last week. There was a store that burned to the ground."

Troy got a sick feeling in his stomach. He said, "What happened? Was anybody injured?"

"There was a lightning storm during the middle of the night. Apparently, the fire was burning enough by the time anybody realized it, that nothing could be done. I am not sure if anybody was injured, but I doubt it. With a fire like that, probably nobody tried to fight it. I hope it was not a friend of yours."

"Thanks, me too. I hope you have a safe trip. Where are you going?"

"I have a friend that lives north of Tucumcari Mountain, so I should be there tomorrow. I hope you have a safe trip also."

Isaac rode on and Troy turned to Don and said, "That scares me to death. What if it was Justine's store and she was injured trying to fight it?"

"Troy, like Isaac said, it was probably too far gone to fight anyway."

"But you know Justine, Don. If anybody would fight for their business, she would."

"Yes, she is a fighter; but she knows she needs to take care of her daughter. And she cannot do that if she is badly injured or dead."

"Don, I sure hope you are right. I do not know what I would do if she was injured badly or killed."

"Troy, we should not even consider those possibilities until we know more about the fire. It might not have been Justine's store at all. We should get back to the caravan and let them know where this crossing is. We can get them safely across the river and to a location to camp for the night. Then we can worry more about the fire and what friend might have lost everything."

"Don, that does not sound very good either. Well, you are right. We should get the wagons across the river. I am not going to stop worrying about Justine."

They got the wagons across the river and settled down for the night. It was another happy night around the camp. The day had gone smoothly, and Albuquerque was only a day or two away.

Don and Troy talked to Armstrong to let him know about the fire in Albuquerque.

Armstrong said, "Wow, Troy, that is too bad. I surely hope that none of your friends were injured. I bet you would like to take off right now and head home."

"I certainly would. But Don has me convinced that since it happened in the middle of the night, probably nobody tried to fight it. And if nobody fought it, nobody would have gotten hurt."

Armstrong said, "Sounds logical to me."

Don said, "If we can get off to a fast start tomorrow, we should be home by the day after."

A fast start did not look like it would be possible by midnight. Another lightning storm sprung up about then. It was just like the storm they suffered through in the canyon. Bolts of lightning were everywhere, and the rain poured like it would never stop.

The caravan had camped for the night on a high spot about two hundred yards west of the river. It was unlikely that the river would rise much. However, everyone was certainly glad they were not camped in a low spot that could flood.

After the storm passed, the drivers checked their animals and found four missing. A half dozen men saddled up and went after the animals. It took them around thirty minutes to return with the escapees. They were all saddle horses, so none of the pulling animals had gotten loose.

Breakfast was a sloppy affair, even though the mess wagon was on high ground. The ground was muddy from the rain. It was decided they would wait until 10:00 a.m. before leaving.

It was clear that the Pecos had risen a good deal, so everyone was glad they had crossed the river the night before. The water was too high for them to cross this morning.

The wagons made slow progress along the muddy trail. By the mid-day break things had started to dry some. The weather looked good, so they would be okay for the rest of this day. Hopefully, they would make it to Albuquerque by tomorrow night. Many hills had been slowing their progress. Nobody knew what the trail would look like the rest of the way home.

By the evening, conditions had improved a great deal. It looked like the trail would continue to be hilly the next day and the weather was still good.

"Troy, how are you holding out," asked Don. "Are you still wanting to make a mad dash for Albuquerque and Justine?"

"More than ever, Don. I am doing my best to hang on. I guess at this point, there really is not much I could do, no matter what the situation is. So, here I sit enjoying a cup of coffee with you. If we do not get there tomorrow evening, we certainly will get there early the next day. If it was Justine's store that burned, I will find her and see what I can do to help. If there is nothing that I can do, then I will make sure my store building is as finished as I am hoping. Then I will start unloading the wagons to start my own store."

Don said, "How are you going to get the wagons unloaded?"

"I will pay the drivers extra to help unload the wagons."

"What is your plan for getting everyone back to New Orleans?"

"I talked to Armstrong about the return trip. They will take all the saddle horses and the chuck wagon. The cook will feed them all the way back to New Orleans. Anybody that wants to leave prior to that is free to go. But. if they stay with the group until they get to New Orleans, Armstrong will pay them a bonus. I arranged that through my banker in New Orleans."

"So, what is your plan about Justine? Are you planning to rush up to her and propose marriage or maybe just some kind of joint venture?"

Troy laughed and said, "A joint venture sounds like a good deal. Maybe I should think of that. If it was her store that burned, she is going to need somewhere to start over. Better with me than some other way. That is an excellent Idea. I really like the sound of it. Justine might be impressed if I asked her about a merger or joint venture."

"Oh, come on, Troy, she is already impressed with you. I do not think you need to suggest a merger. I think you should just propose marriage and be done with it."

"What if she has already forgotten about me and married somebody else?"

"Troy, we have only been gone four months, not four years. How fast do you think she is at falling in love? Of course, I think it only took her several days to fall in love with you; but, I am confident that was an unusual situation.

"Well, maybe we should get to sleep. You will want to look fresh if we get to Albuquerque tomorrow night."

The next morning the caravan started early, and it was good that it did. Almost everything went wrong.

Three saddle horses got loose and had to be chased down.

One wagon broke a wheel and it had to be replaced with a spare that was brought along on the trip.

A driver got bitten by a rattlesnake and had to be treated. He would be alright; but it was a scary incident.

And finally, the chuckwagon ran out of salt for supper.

The good news was that their campsite that night was only a short drive from Albuquerque. The caravan should be in Albuquerque before noon the next day. They had driven as far as they could until dark started to overtake them.

An evening before the conclusion of such a long trip would have called for a celebration. This night everyone just wanted to get to sleep. They would wake in the morning and make their short drive into Albuquerque and the trip would be over. Then they could celebrate.

One person was not sleeping that night and that was Troy Rampy. He laid in his bedroll and just tossed back and forth. He wanted to sleep but could not. All he thought about was Justine. But he would see her tomorrow.

Practically before daylight, the caravan was rolling toward Albuquerque. Everyone grabbed a bite of breakfast, a short cup of coffee and got to their wagons. When the "roll-out" call came, they were ready to move.

The trail was smooth at this point because it had been driven on so many times. Good time was made all morning and by shortly after noon the caravan was rolling into Albuquerque.

Troy and Don took Armstrong to where Troy was hoping his new store would be ready. It was at least on the outside.

Armstrong would guide the caravan to Troy's new store while Troy and Don would look for Justine.

It was sickening to see that the store burned by lightning was Justine's store. Now it was a pile of ashes.

Troy was so anxious to see Justine that Don could barely contain him. They went to her house, and nobody was there. Then they stopped at the hotel, and nobody had seen her. They were able to confirm that she was not injured in the fire.

Several more shops on main street run by friends of hers did not know where she was. But they were certain she was still in town. Finally, someone suggested they go to Aunt Feona's house.

By the time they got across town, the word had already gotten to Justine. Just as Troy and Don were nearing Feona's house, they saw Justine running out the front door.

Justine saw Troy and ran toward him. She practically melted

into his arms as their lips met. She said, "Troy I am so glad to see you. In fact, I am pretty sure I have never been so glad to see anyone in my whole life. How have you been?"

"I have been pretty good, except missing you all the time. How have you been? We saw your store and heard about the lightning storm. I am so glad that you are alright."

"That storm was devastating, but it did not destroy everything. I was remodeling the store and had moved a great deal of merchandise to a safe location." She said that with a wry smile.

Troy said, "Oh, what location?"

Justine smiled again and said, "Well, I know the contractor for your new store. And he let me put my things in there for a while. It looks like it may be longer than I thought now."

Troy smiled a broad grin and said, "I think we should just make it permanent. What would you think of a merger?"

Don, who had been standing back about five feet to give them some space, said, "Troy, it is called a marriage, not a merger."

Troy looked at Justine and said with all seriousness, "What would you think about marrying me?"

Justine, with tears in her eyes, said, "Troy Rampy, I accept your proposal for both the marriage and the merger."

THE END

Made in the USA
Monee, IL
11 June 2025

19236923R00114